Collection Of Ancient Tales

Korean Folk Tales

CHARAN

Some think that love, strong, true, and self-sacrificing, is not to be found in the Orient; but the story of Charan, which comes down four hundred years and more, proves the contrary, for it still has the fresh, sweet flavor of a romance of yesterday; albeit the setting of the East provides an odd and interesting background.

In the days of King Sung-jong (A.D. 1488–1495) one of Korea's noted men became governor of Pyong-an Province. Now Pyong-an stands first of all the eight provinces in the attainments of erudition and polite society. Many of her literati are good musicians, and show ability in the affairs of State.

At the time of this story there was a famous dancing girl in Pyong-an whose name was Charan. She was very beautiful, and sang and danced to the delight of all beholders. Her ability, too, was specially marked, for she understood the classics and was acquainted with history.

The brightest of all the geisha was she, famous and far renowned.

The Governor's family consisted of a son, whose age was sixteen, and whose face was comely as a picture. Though so young, he was thoroughly grounded in Chinese, and was a gifted scholar. His judgment was excellent, and he had a fine appreciation of literary form, so that the moment he lifted his pen the written line took on admirable expression. His name became known as Keydong (The Gifted Lad). The Governor had no other children, neither son nor daughter, so his heart was wrapped up in this boy. On his birthday he had all the officials invited and other special guests, who came to drink his health. There were present also a company of dancing-girls and a large band of musicians. The Governor, during a lull in the banquet, called his son to him, and ordered the chief of the dancing-girls to choose one of the prettiest of their number, that he and she might dance together and delight the assembled guests. On hearing this, the company, with one accord, called for Charan, as the one suited by her talents, attainments and age to be a fitting partner for his son. They came out and danced like fairies, graceful as the wavings of the willow, light and airy as the swallow. All who saw them were charmed. The Governor, too, greatly pleased, called Charan to him, had her sit on the dais, treated her to a share in the banquet, gave her a present of silk, and commanded that from that day forth she be the special dancing maiden to attend upon his son.

From this birthday forth they became fast friends together. They thought the world of each other. More than all the delightful stories of history was their love- such as had never been seen.

The Governor's term of office was extended for six years more, and so they remained in the north country. Finally, at the time of return, he and his wife were in great anxiety over their son being separated from Charan. If they were to force them to separate, they feared he would die of a broken heart. If they took her with them, she not being his wife, they feared for his reputation. They could not possibly decide, so they concluded to refer the matter to the son himself. They called him and said, "Even parents cannot decide as to the love of their son for a maiden. What ought we to do? You love Charan so that it will be very hard for you to part, and yet to have a dancing-girl before you are married is not good form, and will interfere with your marriage prospects and promotion. However, the having of a second wife is a common custom in Korea, and one that the world recognizes. Do as you think best in the matter." The son replied,

"There is no difficulty; when she is before my eyes, of course she is everything, but when the time comes for me to start for home she will be like a pair of worn shoes, set aside; so please do not be anxious."

The Governor and his wife were greatly delighted, and said he was a "superior man" indeed.

When the time came to part Charan cried bitterly, so that those standing by could not bear to look at her; but the son showed not the slightest sign of emotion. Those looking on were filled with wonder at his fortitude. Although he had already loved Charan for six years, he had never been separated from her for a single day, so he knew not what it meant to say Good-bye, nor did he know how it felt to be parted.

The Governor returned to Seoul to fill the office of Chief Justice, and the son came also. After this return thoughts of love for Charan possessed Keydong, though he never expressed them in word or manner. It was almost the time of the Kam-see Examination. The father, therefore, ordered his son to go with some of his friends to a neighboring monastery to study and prepare. They went, and one night, after the day's work was over and all were asleep, the young man stole out into the courtyard. It was winter, with frost and snow and a cold, clear moon. The mountains were deep and the world was quiet, so that the slightest sound could be heard. The young man looked up at the moon and his thoughts were full of sorrow. He so wished to see Charan that he could no longer control himself, and fearing that he would lose his reason, he decided that very night to set out for far-distant Pyong-an. He had on a fur headdress, a thick coat, a leather belt and a heavy pair of shoes. When he had gone less than ten lee, however, his feet were blistered, and he had to go into a neighboring village and change his leather shoes for straw sandals, and his expensive head-cover for an ordinary servant's hat.

He went thus on his way, begging as he went. He was often very hungry, and when night came, was very, very cold. He was a rich man's son and had always dressed in silk and eaten dainty fare, and had never in his life walked more than a few feet from his father's door. Now there lay before him a journey of hundreds of miles. He went stumbling along through the snow, making but poor progress. Hungry, and frozen nearly to death, he had never known such suffering before. His clothes were torn and his face became worn down and blackened till he looked like a goblin. Still on he went, little by little, day after day, till at last, when a whole month had gone by, he reached Pyong-an.

Straight to Charan's home he went, but Charan was not there, only her mother. She looked at him, but did not recognize him. He said he was the former Governor's son and that out of love for Charan he had walked five hundred lee. "Where is she?" he asked.

The mother heard, but instead of being pleased was very angry. She said,

"My daughter is now with the son of the new Governor, and I never see her at all; she never comes home, and she has been away for two or three months. Even though you have made this long journey there is no possible way to meet her."

She did not invite him in, so cold was her welcome. He thought to himself, "I came to see Charan, but she is not here. Her mother refuses me; I cannot go back, and I cannot stay. What shall I do?"

While thus in this dilemma a plan occurred to him. There was a scribe in Pyong-an, who, during his father's term of office, had offended, and was sentenced to death. There were extenuating circumstances, however, and he, when he went to pay his morning

6

salutations, had besought and secured his pardon. His father, out of regard for his son's petition, had forgiven the scribe. He thought, "I was the means of saving the man's life, he will take me in;" so he went straight from Charan's to the house of the scribe. But at first this writer did not recognize him. When he gave his name and told who he was, the scribe gave a great start, and fell at his feet making obeisance. He cleared out an inner room and made him comfortable, prepared dainty fare and treated him with all respect.

A little later he talked over with his host the possibility of his meeting Charan. The scribe said, "I am afraid that there is no way for you to meet her alone, but if you would like to see even her face, I think I can manage it. Will you consent?"

He asked as to the plan. It was this: It being now a time of snow, daily coolies were called to sweep it away from the inner court of the Governor's yamen, and just now the scribe was in charge of this particular work. Said he, "If you will join the sweepers, take a broom and go in; you will no doubt catch a glimpse of Charan as she is said to be in the Hill Kiosk. I know of no other plan."

Keydong consented. In the early morning he mixed with the company of sweepers and went with his broom into the inner enclosure, where the Hill Kiosk was, and so they worked at sweeping. Just then the Governor's son was sitting by the open window and Charan was by him, but not visible from the outside. The other workers, being all practised hands, swept well; Keydong alone handled his broom to no advantage, knowing not how to sweep.

The Governor's son, watching the process, looked out and laughed, called Charan and invited her to see this sweeper.

Charan stepped out into the open hall and the sweeper raised his eyes to see. She glanced at him but once, and but for a moment, then turned quickly, went into the room, and shut the door, not appearing again, to the disappointment of the sweeper, who came back in despair to the scribe's house.

Charan was first of all a wise and highly gifted woman. One look had told her who the sweeper was. She came back into the room and began to cry. The Governor's son looked in surprise and displeasure, and asked, "Why do you cry?"

She did not reply at once, but after two or three insistent demands told the reason this: "I am a low class woman; you are mistaken in thinking highly of me, or counting me of worth. Already I have not been home for two whole months and more. This is a special compliment and a high honor, and so there is not the slightest reason for any complaint on my part. But still, I think of my home, which is poor, and my mother. It is customary on the anniversary of my father's death to prepare food from the official quarters, and offer a sacrifice to his spirit, but here I am imprisoned and to-morrow is the sacrificial day. I fear that not a single act of devotion will be paid, I am disturbed over it, and that's why I cry."

The Governor's son was so taken in by this fair statement that he trusted her fully and without a question. Sympathetically he asked, "Why didn't you tell me before?" He prepared the food and told her to hurry home and carry out the ceremony.

So Charan came like flaming fire back to her house, and said to her mother, "Keydong has come and I have seen him. Is he not here? Tell me where he is if you know." The mother said, "He came here, it is true, all the way on foot to see you, but I told him that you were in the yamen and that there was no possible way for you to meet, so he went away and where he is I know not."

Then Charan broke down and began to cry. "Oh, my mother, why had you the heart to do so cruelly?" she sobbed. "As far as I am concerned I can never break with him nor give him up. We were each sixteen when chosen to dance together, and while it may be said that men chose us, it is truer still to say that God hath chosen. We grew into each other's lives, and there was never such love as ours. Though he forgot and left me, I can never forget and can never give him up. The Governor, too, called me the beloved wife of his son, and did not once refer to my low station. He cherished me and gave me many gifts. It was all like heaven and not like earth. To the city of Pyong-an gentry and officials gather as men crowd into a boat; I have seen so many, but for grace and ability no one was ever like Keydong. I must find him, and even though he casts me aside I never shall forget him. I have not kept myself even unto death as I should have, because I have been under the power and influence of the Governor. How could he ever have come so far for one so low and vile?

He, a gentleman of the highest birth, for the sake of a wretched dancing-girl has endured all this hardship and come so far. Could you not have thought, mother, of these things and given him at least some kindly welcome? Could my heart be other than broken?" And a great flow of tears came from Charan's eyes. She thought and thought as to where he could possibly be. "I know of no place," said she, "unless it be at such and such a scribe's home." Quick as thought she flew thence, and there they met. They clasped each other and cried, not a word was spoken. Thus came they back to Charan's home side by side. When it was night Charan said, "When to-morrow comes we shall have to part. What shall we do?" They talked it over, and agreed to make their escape that night. So Charan got together her clothing, and her treasures and jewels, and made two bundles, and thus, he carrying his on his back and she hers on her head, away they went while the city slept.

They followed the road that leads toward the mountains that lie between Yang-tok and Maing-san counties.

There they found a country house, where they put up, and where the Governor's son became a sort of better-class servant. He did not know how to do anything well, but Charan understood weaving and sewing, and so they lived. After some time they got a little thatched hut by themselves in the village and lived there. Charan was a beautiful sewing-woman, and ceased not day and night to ply her needle, and sold her treasures and her jewels to make ends meet. Charan, too, knew how to make friends, and was praised and loved by all the village. Everybody felt sorry for the hard times that had befallen this mysterious young couple, and helped them so that the days passed peacefully and happily together.

To return in the story: On awaking in the morning in the temple where he and his friends had gone to study, they found Keydong missing. All was in a state of confusion as to what had become of the son of the Chief Justice. They hunted for him far and wide, but he was nowhere to be found, so word was sent to the parents accordingly. There was untold consternation in the home of the former governor. So great a loss, what could equal it?

They searched the country about the temple, but no trace or shadow of him was to be found. Some said they thought he had been inveigled away and metamorphosed by the fox; others that he had been eaten by the tiger. The parents decided that he was dead and went into mourning for him, burning his clothing in a sacrificial fire.

In Pyong-an the Governor's son, when he found that he had lost Charan, had Charan's mother imprisoned and all the relatives, but after a month or so, when the search proved futile, he gave up the matter and let them go.

Charan, at last happy with her chosen one, said one day to him, "You, a son of the gentry, for the sake of a dancing-girl have given up parents and home to live in this hidden corner of the hills. It is a matter, too, that touches your filial piety, this leaving your father and mother in doubt as to whether you are alive or not. They ought to know. We cannot live here all our lives, neither can we return home; what do you think we ought to do?" Keydong made a hopeless reply. "I am in distress," said he, "and know not."

Charan said brightly, "I have a plan by which we can cover over the faults of the past, and win a new start for the future. By means of it, you can serve your parents and look the world in the face. Will you consent?"

"What do you propose?" asked he. Her reply was, "There is only one way, and that is by means of the Official Examination. I know of no other. You will understand what I mean, even though I do not tell you more."

He said, "Enough, your plan is just the thing to help us out. But how can I get hold of the books I need?"

Charan replied, "Don't be anxious about that, I'll get the books." From that day forth she sent through all the neighbourhood for books, to be secured at all costs; but there were few or none, it being a mountain village. One day there came by, all unexpectedly, a pack-peddler, who had in his bundle a book that he wished to sell. Some of the village people wanted to buy it for wall-paper. Charan, however, secured it first and showed it to Keydong. It was none other than a special work for Examinations, with all the exercises written out. It was written in small characters, and was a huge book containing several thousand exercises. Keydong was delighted, and said, "This is enough for all needed preparation." She bought it and gave it to him, and there he pegged away day after day. In the night he studied by candle-light, while she sat by his side and did silk-spinning. Thus they shared the light together. If he showed any remissness, Charan urged him on, and thus they worked for two years. To begin with, he, being a highly talented scholar, made steady advancement day by day. He was a beautiful writer and a master of the pen. His compositions, too, were without a peer, and every indication pointed to his winning the highest place in the Kwago (Examination).

At this time a proclamation was issued that there would be a special examination held before His Majesty the King, so Charan made ready the food required and all necessaries for him to go afoot to Seoul to try his hand.

At last here he was, within the Palace enclosure. His Majesty came out into the examination arena and posted up the subject. Keydong took his pen and wrote his finished composition. Under the inspiration of the moment his lines came forth like bubbling water. It was finished.

When the announcement was made as to the winner, the King ordered the sealed name of the writer to be opened. It was, and they found that Keydong was first. At that time his father was Prime Minister and waiting in attendance upon the King. The King called the Prime Minister, and said, "It looks to me as though the winner was your son, but he writes that his father is Chief Justice and not Prime Minister; what can that mean?" He handed the composition paper to the father, and asked him to look and see. The Minister gazed at it in wonder, burst into tears, and said, "It is your servant's son. Three years ago he went with some friends to a monastery to study, but one night he disappeared, and though I searched far and wide I have had no word of him since. I concluded that he had been destroyed by some wild animal, so I had a funeral service held and the house went into mourning. I had no other children but this son only. He was greatly gifted and I lost him in this strange way. The memory has never left me, for it seems as though I had lost him but yesterday. Now that I look at this paper I see indeed that it is the writing of my son. When I lost him I was Chief Justice, and thus he records the office; but where he has been for these three years, and how he comes now to take part in the examination, I know not."

The King, hearing this, was greatly astonished, and at once before all the assembled ministers had him called. Thus he came in his scholar's dress into the presence of the King.

All the officials wondered at this summoning of a candidate before the announcement of the result.

The King asked him why he had left the monastery and where he had been for these three years. He bowed low, and said, "I have been a very wicked man, have left my parents, have broken all the laws of filial devotion, and deserve condign punishment."

The King replied, saying, "There is no law of concealment before the King. I shall not condemn you even though you are guilty; tell me all." Then he told his story to the King.

All the officials on each side bent their ears to hear. The King sighed, and said to the father, "Your son has repented and made amends for his fault. He has won first place and now stands as a member of the Court. We cannot condemn him for his love for this woman. Forgive him for all the past and give him a start for the future." His Majesty said further, "The woman Charan, who has shared your life in the lonely mountains, is no common woman. Her plans, too, for your restoration were the plans of a master hand. She is no dancing-girl, this Charan. Let no other be your lawful wife but she only; let her be raised to equal rank with her husband, and let her children and her children's children hold highest office in the realm." So was Keydong honored with the winner's crown, and so the Prime Minister received his son back to life at the hands of the King. The winner's cap was placed upon his head, and the whole house was whirled into raptures of joy.

So the Minister sent forth a palanquin and servants to bring up Charan. In a great festival of joy she was proclaimed the wife of the Minister's son. Later he became one of Korea's first men of State, and they lived their happy life to a good old age. They had two sons, both graduates and men who held high office.

THE STORY OF
CHANG TO-RYONG

Taoism has been one of the great religions of Korea. Its main thought is expressed in the phrase su-sim yon-song, "to correct the mind and reform the nature"; while Buddhism's is myong-sim kyon-song, "to enlighten the heart and see the soul."

The desire of all Taoists is "eternal life," chang-saing pul-sa; that of the Buddhists, to rid oneself of fleshly being. In the Taoist world of the genii, there are three great divisions: the upper genii, who live with God; the midway genii, who have to do with the world of angels and spirits; and the lower genii, who rule in sacred places on the earth, among the hills, just as we find in the story of Chang To-ryong.

In the days of King Chung-jong (A.D. 1507–1526) there lived a beggar in Seoul, whose face was extremely ugly and always dirty. He was forty years of age or so, but still wore his hair down his back like an unmarried boy. He carried a bag over his shoulder, and went about the streets begging. During the day he went from one part of the city to the other, visiting each section, and when night came on he would huddle up beside some one's gate and go to sleep. He was frequently seen in Chong-no (Bell Street) in company with the servants and underlings of the rich. They were great friends, he and they, joking and bantering as they met. He used to say that his name was Chang, and so they called him Chang To-ryong, To-ryong meaning an unmarried boy, son of the gentry. At that time the magician Chon U-chi, who was far-famed for his pride and arrogance, whenever he met Chang, in passing along the street, would dismount and prostrate himself most humbly. Not only did he bow, but he seemed to regard Chang with the greatest of fear, so that he dared not look him in the face. Chang, sometimes, without even inclining his head, would say, "Well, how goes it with you, eh?" Chon, with his hands in his sleeves, most respectfully would reply, "Very well, sir, thank you, very well." He had fear written on all his features when he faced Chang.

Sometimes, too, when Chon would bow, Chang would refuse to notice him at all, and go by without a word. Those who saw it were astonished, and asked Chon the reason. Chon said in reply, "There are only three spirit-men at present in Cho-sen, of whom the greatest is Chang To-ryong; the second is Cheung Puk-chang; and the third is Yun Se-pyong. People of the world do not know it, but I do. Such being the case, should I not bow before him and show him reverence?"

Those who heard this explanation, knowing that Chon himself was a strange being, paid no attention to it.

At that time in Seoul there was a certain literary undergraduate in office whose house joined hard on the street. This man used to see Chang frequently going about begging, and one day he called him and asked who he was, and why he begged. Chang made answer, "I was originally of a cultured family of Chulla Province, but my parents died of typhus fever, and I had no brothers or relations left to share my lot. I alone remained of all my clan, and having no home of my own I have gone about begging, and have at last reached Seoul. As I am not skilled in any handicraft, and do not know Chinese letters, what else can I do?" The undergraduate, hearing that he was a scholar, felt very sorry for him, gave him food and drink, and refreshed him.

From this time on, whenever there was any special celebration at his home, he used to call Chang in and have him share it.

On a certain day when the master was on his way to office, he saw a dead body being carried on a stretcher off toward the Water Gate. Looking at it closely from the horse on which he rode, he recognized it as the corpse of Chang To-ryong. He felt so sad that he turned back to his house and cried over it, saying, "There are lots of miserable people on earth, but who ever saw one as miserable as poor Chang? As I reckon the time over on my fingers, he has been begging in Bell Street for fifteen years, and now he passes out of the city a dead body."

Twenty years and more afterwards the master had to make a journey through South Chulla Province. As he was passing Chi-i Mountain, he lost his way and got into a maze among the hills. The day began to wane, and he could neither return nor go forward. He saw a narrow footpath, such as woodmen take, and turned into it to see if it led to any habitation. As he went along there were rocks and deep ravines. Little by little, as he advanced farther, the scene changed and seemed to become strangely transfigured. The farther he went the more wonderful it became. After he had gone some miles he discovered himself to be in another world entirely, no longer a world of earth and dust.

He saw someone coming toward him dressed in ethereal green, mounted and carrying a shade, with servants accompanying. He seemed to sweep toward him with swiftness and without effort. He thought to himself, "Here is some high lord or other coming to meet me, but," he added, "how among these deeps and solitudes could a gentleman come riding so?" He led his horse aside and tried to withdraw into one of the groves by the side of the way, but before he could think to turn the man had reached him.

The mysterious stranger lifted his two hands in salutation and inquired respectfully as to how he had been all this time. The master was speechless, and so astonished that he could make no reply. But the stranger smilingly said, "My house is quite near here; come with me and rest."

He turned, and leading the way seemed to glide and not to walk, while the master followed. At last they reached the place indicated. He suddenly saw before him great palace halls filling whole squares of space. Beautiful buildings they were, richly ornamented. Before the door attendants in official robes awaited them.

They bowed to the master and led him into the hall. After passing a number of gorgeous, palace-like rooms, he arrived at a special one and ascended to the upper storey, where he met a very wonderful person. He was dressed in shining garments, and the servants that waited on him were exceedingly fair. There were, too, children about, so exquisitely beautiful that it seemed none other than a celestial palace. The master, alarmed at finding himself in such a place, hurried forward and made a low obeisance, not daring to lift his eyes. But the host smiled upon him, raised his hands and asked, "Do you not know me? Look now." Lifting his eyes, he then saw that it was the same person who had come riding out to meet him, but he could not tell who he was. "I see you," said he, "but as to who you are I cannot tell."

The kingly host then said, "I am Chang To-ryong. Do you not know me?" Then as the master looked more closely at him he could see the same features. The outlines of the face were there, but all the imperfections had gone, and only beauty remained. So wonderful was it that he was quite overcome.

A great feast was prepared, and the honored guest was entertained. Such food, too, was placed before him as was never seen on earth. Angelic beings played on beautiful instruments and danced as no mortal eye ever looked upon. Their faces, too, were like pearls and precious stones.

Chang To-ryong said to his guest, "There are four famous mountains in Korea in which the genii reside. This hill is one. In days gone by, for a fault of mine, I was exiled to earth, and in the time of my exile you treated me with marked kindness, a favor that I have never forgotten.

When you saw my dead body your pity went out to me; this, too, I remember. I was not dead then, it was simply that my days of exile were ended and I was returning home. I knew that you were passing this hill, and I desired to meet you and to thank you for all your kindness. Your treatment of me in another world is sufficient to bring about our meeting in this one." And so they met and feasted in joy and great delight.

When night came he was escorted to a special pavilion, where he was to sleep. The windows were made of jade and precious stones, and soft lights came streaming through them, so that there was no night. "My body was so rested and my soul so refreshed," said he, "that I felt no need of sleep."

When the day dawned a new feast was spread, and then farewells were spoken. Chang said, "This is not a place for you to stay long in; you must go. The ways differ of we genii and you men of the world. It will be difficult for us ever to meet again. Take good care of yourself and go in peace." He then called a servant to accompany him and show the way. The master made a low bow and withdrew. When he had gone but a short distance he suddenly found himself in the old world with its dusty accompaniments. The path by which he came out was not the way by which he had entered. In order to mark the entrance he planted a stake, and then the servant withdrew and disappeared.

The year following the master went again and tried to find the citadel of the genii, but there were only mountain peaks and impassable ravines, and where it was he never could discover.

As the years went by the master seemed to grow younger in spirit, and at last at the age of ninety he passed away without suffering. "When Chang was here on earth and I saw him for fifteen years," said the master, "I remember but one peculiarity about him, namely, that his face never grew older nor did his dirty clothing ever wear out. He never changed his garb, and yet it never varied in appearance in all the fifteen years. This alone would have marked him as a strange being, but our fleshly eyes did not recognize it."

A STORY OF THE FOX

The Fox. Orientals say that among the long-lived creatures are the tortoise, the deer, the crane and the fox, and that these long-lived ones attain to special states of spiritual refinement. If trees exist through long ages they become coal; if pine resin endures it becomes amber; so the fox, if it lives long, while it never becomes an angel, or spiritual being, as a man does, takes on various metamorphoses, and appears on earth in various forms.

Yi Kwai was the son of a minister. He passed his examinations and held high office. When his father was Governor of Pyong-an Province, Kwai was a little boy and accompanied him. The Governor's first wife being dead, Kwai's stepmother was the mistress of the home.

Once when His Excellency had gone out on an inspecting tour, the yamen was left vacant, and Kwai was there with her. In the rear garden of the official quarters was a pavilion, called the Hill Pagoda, that connected by a narrow gateway with the public hall. Frequently Kwai took one of the yamen boys with him and went there to study, and once at night when it had grown late and the boy who accompanied him had taken his departure, the door opened suddenly and a young woman came in. Her clothes were neat and clean, and she was very pretty. Kwai looked carefully at her, but did not recognize her. She was evidently a stranger, as there was no such person among the dancing-girls of the men.

He remained looking at her, in doubt as to who she was, while she on the other hand took her place in the corner of the room and said nothing.

"Who are you?" he asked. She merely laughed and made no reply. He called her. She came and knelt down before him, and he took her by the hand and patted her shoulder, as though he greeted her favorably. The woman smiled and pretended to enjoy it. He concluded, however, that she was not a real woman, but a goblin of some kind, or perhaps a fox, and what to do he knew not. Suddenly he decided on a plan, caught her, swung her on to his back, and rushed out through the gate into the yamen quarters, where he shouted at the top of his voice for his stepmother and the servants to come.

It was midnight and all were asleep. No one replied, and no one came. The woman, then, being on his back, bit him furiously at the nape of the neck. By this he knew that she was the fox. Unable to stand the pain of it, he loosened his grasp, when she jumped to the ground, made her escape and was seen no more.

What a pity that no one came to Kwai's rescue and so made sure of the beast!

CHEUNG PUK-CHANG, THE SEER

Cheung Puk-chang.- The Yol-ryok Keui-sul, one of Korea's noted histories, says of Cheung Puk-chang that he was pure in purpose and without selfish ambition. He was superior to all others in his marvelous gifts. For him to read a book once was to know it by heart. There was nothing that he could not understand- astronomy, geology, music, medicine, mathematics, fortune-telling and Chinese characters, which he knew by intuition and not from study.

He followed his father in the train of the envoy to Peking, and there talked to all the strange peoples whom he met without any preparation. They all wondered at him and called him "The Mystery." He knew, too, the meaning of the calls of birds and beasts; and while he lived in the mountains he could see and tell what people were doing in the distant valley, indicating what was going on in each house, which, upon investigation, was found in each case to be true. He was a Taoist, and received strange revelations.

While in Peking there met him envoys from the Court of Loochoo, who also were prophets. While in their own country they had studied the horoscope, and on going into

China knew that they were to meet a Holy Man. As they went on their way they asked concerning this mysterious being, and at last reached Peking. Inquiring, they went from one envoy's station to another till they met Cheung Puk-chang, when a great fear came upon them, and they fell prostrate to the earth.

They took from their baggage a little book inscribed, "In such a year, on such a day, at such an hour, in such a place, you shall meet a Holy Man." "If this does not mean your Excellency," said they, "whom can it mean?" They asked that he would teach them the sacred Book of Changes, and he responded by teaching it in their own language. At that time the various envoys, hearing of this, contended with each other as to who should first see the marvelous stranger, and he spoke to each in his own tongue. They all, greatly amazed, said, "He is indeed a man of God."

Some one asked him, saying, "There are those who understand the sounds of birds and beasts, but foreign languages have to be learned to be known; how can you speak them without study?"

Puk-chang replied, "I do not know them from having learned them, but know them unconsciously."

Puk-chang was acquainted with the three religions, but he considered Confucianism as the first. "Its writings as handed down," said he, "teach us filial piety and reverence. The learning of the Sages deals with relationships among men and not with spiritual mysteries; but Taoism and Buddhism deal with the examination of the soul and the heart, and so with things above and not with things on the earth. This is the difference."

At thirty-two years of age he matriculated, but had no interest in further literary study. He became, instead, an official teacher of medicine, astrology and mathematics.

He was a fine whistler, we are told, and once when he had climbed to the highest peak of the Diamond Mountains and there whistled, the echoes resounded through the hills, and the priests were startled and wondered whose flute was playing.

There is a term in Korea which reads he-an pang-kwang, "spiritual-eye distant-vision," the seeing of things in the distance. This pertains to both Taoists and Buddhists.

It is said that when the student reaches a certain stage in his progress, the soft part of the head returns to the primal thinness that is seen in the child to rise and fall when it breathes. From this part of the head go forth five rays of light that shoot out and up more and more as the student advances in the spiritual way. As far as they extend so is the spiritual vision perfected, until at last a Korean sufficiently advanced could sit and say, "In London, to-day, such and such a great affair is taking place."

For example, So Wha-tam, who was a Taoist Sage, once was seen to laugh to himself as he sat with closed eyes, and when asked why he laughed, said, "Just now in the monastery of Ha-in (300 miles distant) there is a great feast going on. The priest stirring the huge kettle of bean gruel has tumbled in, but the others do not know this, and are eating the soup." News came from the monastery later on that proved that what the sage had seen was actually true.

The History of Confucius, too, deals with this when it tells of his going with his disciple An-ja and looking off from the Tai Mountains of Shan-tung toward the kingdom of On. Confucius asked An-ja if he could see anything, and An-ja replied, "I see white horses tied at the gates of On."

Confucius said, "No, no, your vision is imperfect, desist from looking. They are not white horses, but are rolls of white silk hung out for bleaching."

The Story

The Master, Puk-chang, was a noted Korean. From the time of his birth he was a wonderful mystery. In reading a book, if he but glanced through it, he could recall it word for word. Without any special study he became a master of astronomy, geology, medicine, fortune-telling, music, mathematics and geomancy, and so truly a specialist was he that he knew them all.

He was thoroughly versed also in the three great religions, Confucianism, Buddhism, and Taoism. He talked constantly of what other people could not possibly comprehend. He understood the sounds of the birds, the voices of Nature, and much else. He accompanied his father in his boyhood days when he went as envoy to Peking. At that time, strange barbarian peoples used also to come and pay their tribute. Puk-chang picked up acquaintance with them on the way. Hearing their language but once, he was readily able to communicate with them. His own countrymen who accompanied him were not the only ones astonished, nor the Chinamen themselves, but the barbarians as well. There are numerous interesting stories hinted at in the history of Puk-chang, but few suitable records were made of them, and so many are lost.

There is one, however, that I recall that comes to me through trustworthy witnesses: Puk-chang, on a certain day, went to visit his paternal aunt. She asked him to be seated, and as they talked together, said to him, "I had some harvesting to do in Yong-nam County, and sent a servant to see to it. His return is overdue and yet he does not come. I am afraid he has fallen in with thieves, or chanced on a fire or some other misfortune."

Puk-chang replied, "Shall I tell you how it goes with him, and how far he has come on the way?"

She laughed, saying, "Do you mean to joke about it?"

Puk-chang, from where he was sitting, looked off apparently to the far south, and at last said to his aunt, "He is just now crossing the hill called Bird Pass in Mun-kyong County, Kyong-sang Province. Hallo! he is getting a beating just now from a passing yangban (gentleman), but I see it is his own fault, so you need not trouble about him."

The aunt laughed, and asked, "Why should he be beaten; what's the reason, pray?"

Puk-chang replied, "It seems this official was eating his dinner at the top of the hill when your servant rode by him without dismounting. The gentleman was naturally very angry and had his servants arrest your man, pull him from his horse, and beat him over the face with their rough straw shoes."

The aunt could not believe it true, but treated the matter as a joke; and yet Puk-chang did not seem to be joking.

Interested and curious, she made a note of the day on the wall after Puk-chang had taken his departure, and when the servant returned, she asked him what day he had come over Bird Pass, and it proved to be the day recorded. She added also, "Did you get into trouble with a yangban there when you came by?"

The servant gave a startled look, and asked, "How do you know?" He then told all that had happened to him, and it was just as Puk-chang had given it even to the smallest detail.

YUN SE-PYONG, THE WIZARD

Yun Se-pyong was a man of Seoul who lived to the age of over ninety. When he was young he loved archery, and went as military attaché to the capital of the Mings (Nanking). There he met a prophet who taught him the Whang-jong Kyong, or Sacred Book of the Taoists, and thus he learned their laws and practised their teachings. His life was written by Yi So-kwang.

Chon U-chi was a magician of Songdo who lived about 1550, and was associated in his life with Shin Kwang-hu. At the latter's residence one day when a friend called, Kwang-hu asked Chon to show them one of his special feats. A little later they brought in a table of rice for each of the party, and Chon took a mouthful of his, and then blew it out toward the courtyard, when the rice changed into beautiful butterflies that flew gaily away.

Chang O-sa used to tell a story of his father, who said that one day Chon came to call upon him at his house and asked for a book entitled The Tu-si, which he gave to him. "I had no idea," said the father, "that he was dead and that it was his ghost. I gave him the book, though I did not learn till afterwards that he had been dead for a long time."

The History of Famous Men says, "He was a man who understood heretical magic, and other dangerous teachings by which he deceived the people. He was arrested for this and locked up in prison in Sin-chon, Whanghai Province, and there he died. His burial was ordered by the prison authorities, and later, when his relatives came to exhume his remains, they found that the coffin was empty."

This and the story of do not agree as to his death, and I am not able to judge between them.

The transformation of men into beasts, bugs and creeping things comes from Buddhism; one seldom finds it in Taoism.

The Story

Yun Se-Pyong was a military man who rose to the rank of minister in the days of King Choong-jong. It seems that Yun learned the doctrine of magic from a passing stranger, whom he met on his way to Peking in company with the envoy. When at home he lived in a separate house, quite apart from the other members of his family. He was a man so greatly feared that even his wife and children dared not approach him. What he did in secret no one seemed to know. In winter he was seen to put iron cleats under each arm and to change them frequently, and when they were put off they seemed to be red-hot.

At the same time there was a magician in Korea called Chon U-chi, who used to go about Seoul plying his craft. So skilful was he that he could even simulate the form of the master of a house and go freely into the women's quarters. On this account he was greatly feared and detested. Yun heard of him on more than one occasion, and determined to rid the earth of him. Chon heard also of Yun and gave him a wide berth, never appearing in his presence. He used frequently to say, "I am a magician only; Yun is a God."

On a certain day Chon informed his wife that Yun would come that afternoon and try to kill him, "and so," said he, "I shall change my shape in order to escape his clutches. If any one comes asking for me just say that I am not at home." He then metamorphosed himself into a beetle, and crawled under a crock that stood overturned in the courtyard.

When evening began to fall a young woman came to Chon's house, a very beautiful woman too, and asked, "Is the master Chon at home?"

The wife replied, "He has just gone out."

The woman laughingly said, "Master Chon and I have been special friends for a long time, and I have an appointment with him to-day. Please say to him that I have come."

Chon's wife, seeing a pretty woman come thus, and ask in such a familiar way for her husband, flew into a rage and said, "The rascal has evidently a second wife that he has never told me of. What he said just now is all false," so she went out in a fury, and with a club smashed the crock. When the crock was broken there was the beetle underneath it. Then the woman who had called suddenly changed into a bee, and flew at and stung the beetle. Chon, metamorphosed into his accustomed form, fell over and died, and the bee flew away.

Yun lived at his own house as usual, when suddenly he broke down one day in a fit of tears. The members of his family in alarm asked the reason.

He replied, "My sister living in Chulla Province has just at this moment died." He then called his servants, and had them prepare funeral supplies, saying, "They are poor where she lives, and so I must help them."

He wrote a letter, and after sealing it, said to one of his attendants, "If you go just outside the gate you will meet a man wearing a horsehair cap and a soldier's uniform. Call him in. He is standing there ready to be summoned."

He was called in, and sure enough he was a Kon-yun-no (servant of the gods). He came in and at once prostrated himself before Yun. Yun said, "My sister has just now died in such a place in Chulla Province. Take this letter and go at once. I shall expect you back to-night with the answer. The matter is of such great importance that if you do not bring it as I order, and within the time appointed, I shall have you punished."

He replied, "I shall be in time, be not anxious."

Yun then gave him the letter and the bundle, and he went outside the main gateway and disappeared.

Before dark he returned with the answer. The letter read: "She died at such an hour to-day and we were in straits as to what to do, when your letter came with the supplies, just as though we had seen each other. Wonderful it is!" The man who brought the answer immediately went out and disappeared. The house of mourning is situated over ten days' journey from Seoul, but he returned ere sunset, in the space of two or three hours.

THE WILD-CAT WOMAN

Kim Su-ik was a native of Seoul who matriculated in 1624 and graduated in 1630. In 1636, when the King made his escape to Nam-han from the invading Manchu army, Kim Su-ik accompanied him. He opposed any yielding to China or any treaty with them, but because his counsel was not received he withdrew from public life.

Tong Chung-so was a Chinaman of great note. He once desired to give himself up to study, and did not go out of his room for three years. During this time a young man one day called on him, and while he stood waiting said to himself, "It will rain to-day." Tong replied at once, "If you are not a fox you are a wild cat- out of this," and the man at once ran away. How he came to know this was from the words, "Birds that live in the trees know when the wind will blow; beasts that live in the ground know when it is going to rain." The wild cat unconsciously told on himself.

The Story

The former magistrate of Quelpart, Kim Su-ik, lived inside of the South Gate of Seoul. When he was young it was his habit to study Chinese daily until late at night. Once, when feeling hungry, he called for his wife to bring him something to eat.

The wife replied, "We have nothing in the house except seven or eight chestnuts. Shall I roast these and bring them to you?"

Kim replied, "Good; bring them."

The servants were asleep, and there was no one on hand to answer a call, so the wife went to the kitchen, made a fire and cooked them herself. Kim waited, meanwhile, for her to come.

After a little while she brought them in a hand basket, cooked and ready served for him. Kim ate and enjoyed them much. Meanwhile she sat before his desk and waited. Suddenly the door opened, and another person entered. Kim raised his eyes to see, and there was the exact duplicate of his wife, with a basket in her hand and roasted chestnuts. As he looked at both of them beneath the light the two women were perfect facsimiles of each other. The two also looked back and forth in alarm, saying, "What's this that's happened? Who are you?"

Kim once again received the roasted nuts, laid them down, and then took firm hold of each woman, the first one by the right hand and the second by the left, holding fast till the break of day.

At last the cock's crew, and the east began to lighten. The one whose right hand he held, said, "Why do you hold me so? It hurts; let me go." She shook and tugged, but Kim held all the tighter. In a little, after struggling, she fell to the floor and suddenly changed into a wild cat. Kim, in fear and surprise, let her go, and she made her escape through the door. What a pity that he did not make the beast fast for good and all!

Note by the writer- Foxes turning into women and deceiving people is told of in Kwang-keui and other Chinese novels, but the wild cat's transformation is more wonderful still, and something that I have never heard of. By what law do creatures like foxes and wild cats so change? I am unable to find any law that governs it. Some say that the fox carries a magic charm by which it does these magic things, but can this account for the wild cat?

THE ILL-FATED PRIEST

A certain scribe of Chung-chong Province, whose name was Kim Kyong-jin, once told me the following story. Said he: "In the year 1640, as I was journeying past Big Horn Bridge in Ta-in County, I saw a scholar, who, with his four or five servants, had met with some accident and all were reduced to a state of unconsciousness, lying by the river side. I asked the reason for what had befallen them, and they at last said in reply, 'We were eating our noon meal by the side of the road, when a Buddhist priest came by, a proud, arrogant fellow, who refused to bow or show any recognition of us. One of the servants, indignant at this, shouted at him. The priest, however, beat him with his stick, and when others went to help, he beat them also, so that they were completely worsted and unable to rise or walk. He then scolded the scholar, saying, "You did not reprimand your servants for their insult to me, so I'll have to take it out of you as well." The Buddhist gave him a number of vicious lows, so that he completely collapsed;' and when I looked there was the priest a li or two ahead.

"Just then a military man, aged about forty or so, came my way. He was poor in flesh and seemed to have no strength. Riding a cadaverous pony, he came shuffling along; a boy accompanying carried his hat-cover and bow and arrows. He arrived at the stream, and, seeing the people in their plight, asked the cause. The officer was very angry, and said, 'Yonder impudent priest, endowed with no end of brute force, has attacked my people and me.'

"'Indeed,' said the stranger, 'I have been aware of him for a long time, and have decided to rid the earth of him, but I have never had an opportunity before. Now that I have at last come on him I am determined to have satisfaction.' So he dismounted from his horse, tightened his girth, took his bow, and an arrow that had a 'fist' head, and made off at a gallop after the priest. Soon he overtook him. Just as the priest looked back the archer let fly with his arrow, which entered deep into the chest. He then dismounted, drew his sword, pierced the two hands of the priest and passed a string through them, tied him to his horse's tail, and came triumphantly back to where the scholar lay, and said, 'Now do with this fellow as you please. I am going.'

"The scholar bowed before the archer, thanked him, asked his place of residence and name. He replied, 'My home is in the County of Ko-chang,' but he did not give his name.

"The scholar looked at the priest, and never before had he seen so powerful a giant, but now, with his chest shot through and his hands pierced, he was unable to speak; so they arose, made mincemeat of him, and went on their way rejoicing."

THE VISION OF THE HOLY MAN

Yi Chi-Ham (Master To-jong).- A story is told of him that on the day after his wedding he went out with his topo or ceremonial coat on, but came back later without it. On inquiry being made, it was found that he had torn it into pieces to serve as bandages for a sick child that he had met with on his walk.

Once on a time he had an impression that his father-in-law's home was shortly to be overtaken by a great disaster; he therefore took his wife and disappeared from the place. In the year following, for some political offence, the home was indeed wiped out and the family wholly destroyed.

To-jong was not only a prophet, but also a magician, as was shown by his handling of a boat. When he took to sea the waters lay quiet before him, and all his path was peace. He would be absent sometimes for a year or more, voyaging in many parts of the world.

He practised fasting, and would go sometimes for months without eating. He also overcame thirst, and in the hot days of summer would avoid drinking. He stifled all pain and suffering, so that when he walked and his feet were blistered he paid no attention to it.

While young he was a disciple of a famous Taoist, So Wha-dam. As his follower he used to dress in grass cloth (the poor man's garb), wear straw shoes and carry his bundle on his back. He would be on familiar terms with Ministers of State, and yet show indifference to their greatness and pomp. He was acquainted with the various magic practices, so that in boating he used to hang out gourd cups at each corner of the boat, and thus equipped he went many times to and from Quelpart and never met a wind. He did merchandising, made money, and bought land, which yielded several thousand bags of rice that he distributed among the poor.

He lived in Seoul in a little dug-out, so that his name became "Mud Pavilion," or To-jong. His cap was made of metal, which he used to cook his food in, and which he then washed and put back on his head again. He used also to wear wooden shoes and ride on a pack saddle.

He built a house for the poor in Asan County when he was magistrate there, gathered in all the needy and had them turn to and work at whatever they had any skill in, so that they lived and flourished. When any one had no special ability, he had him weave straw shoes. He urged them on till they could make as many as ten pairs a day.

Yul-gok said of him that he was a dreamer and not suitable for this matter-of-fact world, because he belonged to the realm of flowers and pretty birds, songs and sweet breezes, and not to the common clay of corn and beef and radishes. To-jong heard this, and replied, "Though I am not of a kind equal to beans and corn, still I will rank with acorns and chestnuts. Why am I wholly useless?"

The Story

Teacher To-jong was once upon a time a merchant, and in his merchandising went as far as the East Sea. One night he slept in a fishing village on the shore. At that time another stranger called who was said to be an i-in or "holy man." The three met and talked till late at night- the master of the house, the "holy man" and To-jong. It was very clear and beautifully calm. The "holy man" looked for a time out over the expanse of water, then suddenly gave a great start of terror, and said, "An awful thing is about to happen."

His companions, alarmed at his manner, asked him what he meant. He replied, "In two hours or so there will be a tidal wave that will engulf this whole village, utterly destroying everything. If you do not make haste to escape all will be as fish in a net."

To-jong, being something of an astrologer himself, thought first to solve the mystery of this, but could arrive at no explanation.

The owner of the house would not believe it, and refused to prepare for escape.

The "holy man" said, however, "Even though you do not believe what I say, let us go for a little up the face of the rear mountain.

If my words fail we can only come down again, and no one will be the worse for it. If you still do not wish to trust me, leave your goods and furniture just as they are and let the people come away."

To-jong was greatly interested, though he could not understand it. The master, too, could no longer refuse this proposal, so he took his family and a few light things and followed the "holy man" up the hill.

He had them ascend to the very top, "in order," said he, "to escape."

To-jong did not go to the top, but seated himself about half-way up. He asked the "holy man" if he would not be safe enough there.

The "holy man" replied, "Others would never escape if they remained where you are, but you will simply get a fright and live through it."

When cock-crow came, sure enough the sea suddenly lifted its face, overflowed its banks, and the waves came rolling up to the heavens, climbing the mountain-sides till they touched the feet of To-jong. The whole town on the seashore was engulfed. When daylight came the waters receded.

To-jong bowed to the "holy man" and asked that he might become his disciple. The "holy man," however, disclaimed any knowledge, saying that he had simply known it by accident. He was a man who did not speak of his own attainments. To-jong asked for his place of residence, which he indicated as nearby, and then left. He went to seek him on the following day, but the house was vacant, and there was no one there.

THE VISIT OF THE MAN OF GOD

In the thirty-third year of Mal-yok of the Mings (A.D. 1605), being the year Eulsa of the reign of Son-jo, in the seventh moon, a great rain fell, such a rain as had not been seen since the founding of the dynasty. Before that rain came on, a man of Kang-won Province was cutting wood on the hill-side. While thus engaged, an angel in golden armor, riding on a white horse and carrying a spear, came down to him from heaven. His appearance was most dazzling, and the woodman, looking at him, recognized him as a Man of God. Also a Buddhist priest, carrying a staff, came down in his train. The priest's appearance, too, was very remarkable.

The Man of God stopped his horse and seemed to be talking with the priest, while the woodcutter, alarmed by the great sight, hid himself among the trees.

The Man of God seemed to be very angry for some reason or other, raised his spear, and, pointing to the four winds, said, "I shall flood all the earth from such a point to such a point, and destroy the inhabitants thereof."

The priest following cried and prayed him to desist, saying, "This will mean utter destruction to mortals; please let thy wrath rest on me." As he prayed thus earnestly the Man of God again said, "Then shall I limit it to such and such places. Will that do?"

But the priest prayed more earnestly still, till the Man replied emphatically, "I have lessened the punishment more than a half already on your account; I can do no more." Though the priest prayed still, the Man of God refused him, so that at last he submissively said, "Thy will be done."

They ended thus and both departed, passing away through the upper air into heaven.

The two had talked for a long time, but the distance being somewhat great between them and the woodman, he did not hear distinctly all that was said.

He went home, however, in great haste, and with his wife and family made his escape, and from that day the rain began to fall. In it Mount Otai collapsed, the earth beneath it sank until it became a vast lake, all the inhabitants were destroyed, and the woodcutter alone made his escape.

THE LITERARY MAN OF IMSIL

The calling of spirits is one of the powers supposed to be possessed by disciples of the Old Philosopher (Taoists), who reach a high state of spiritual attainment. While the natural desires remain they cloud and obstruct spiritual vision; once rid of them, even angels and immortal beings become unfolded to the sight. They say, "If once all the obstructions of the flesh are eliminated even God can be seen." They also say, "If I have no selfish desire, the night around me will shine with golden light; and if all injurious thoughts are truly put away, the wild deer of the mountain will come down and play beside me."

Ha Sa-gong, a Taoist of high attainment, as an old man used to go out fishing, when the pigeons would settle in flights upon his head and shoulders. On his return one day he told his wife that they were so many that they bothered him. "Why not catch one of them?" said his wife. "Catch one?" said he. "What would you do with it?" "Why, eat it, of course." So on the second day Ha went out with this intent in heart, but no birds came near or alighted on him. All kept a safe distance high up in mid-air, with doubt and suspicion evident in their flying.

The Story

In the year 1654 there was a man of letters living in Imsil who claimed that he could control spirits, and that two demon guards were constantly at his bidding. One day he was sitting with a friend playing chess, when they agreed that the loser in each case was to pay a fine in drink. The friend lost and yet refused to pay his wager, so that the master said, "If you do not pay up I'll make it hot for you." The man, however, refused, till at last the master, exasperated, turned his back upon him and called out suddenly into the upper air some formula or other, as if he were giving a command. The man dashed off through the courtyard to make his escape, but an unseen hand bared his body, and administered to him such a set of sounding blows that they left blue, seamy marks. Unable to bear the pain of it longer, he yielded, and then the master laughed and let him go.

At another time he was seated with a friend, while in the adjoining village a witch koot (exorcising ceremony) was in progress, with drums and gongs banging furiously. The master suddenly rushed out to the bamboo grove that stood behind the official yamen, and, looking very angry and with glaring eyes, he shouted, and made bare his arm as if to drive off the furies. After a time he ceased. The friend, thinking this a peculiar performance, asked what it meant. His reply was, "A crowd of devils have come from the koot, and are congregating in the grove of bamboos; if I do not drive them off trouble will follow in the town, and for that cause I shouted."

Again he was making a journey with a certain friend, when suddenly, on the way, he called out to the mid-air, saying, "Let her go, let her go, I say, or I'll have you punished severely."

His appearance was so peculiar and threatening that the friend asked the cause. For the time being he gave no answer, and they simply went on their way.

That night they entered a village where they wished to sleep, but the owner of the house where they applied said that they had sickness, and asked them to go. They insisted, however, till he at last sent a servant to drive them off. Meanwhile the womenfolk watched the affair through the chinks of the window, and they talked in startled whispers, so that the scholar overheard them.

A few minutes later the man of the house followed in the most humble and abject manner, asking them to return and accept entertainment and lodging at his house. Said he, "I have a daughter, sir, and she fell ill this very day and died, and after some time came to life again. Said she, 'A devil caught me and carried my soul off down the main roadway, where we met a man, who stopped us, and in fierce tones drove off the spirit, who let me go, and so I returned to life.' She looked out on your Excellency through the chink of the window, and, behold, you are the man. I am at my wits' end to know what to say to you. Are you a genii or are you a Buddhist, so marvelously to bring back the dead to life? I offer this small refreshment; please accept."

The scholar laughed, and said, "Nonsense! Just a woman's have rings. How could I do such things?" He lived for seven or eight years more, and died.

THE SOLDIER OF KANG-WHA

The East says that the air is full of invisible constituents that, once taken in hand and controlled, will take on various forms of life. The man of Kang-wha had acquired the art of calling together the elements necessary for the butterfly. This, too, comes from Taoism, and is called son-sul, Taoist magic

The Story

There was a soldier once of Kang-wha who was the chief man of his village; a low-class man, he was, apparently, without any gifts. One day his wife, overcome by a fit of jealousy, sat sewing in her inner room. It was midwinter, and he was obliged to be at home; so, with intent to cheer her up and take her mind off the blues, he said to her, "Would you like to see me make some butterflies?"

His wife, more angry than ever at this, rated him for his impudence, and paid no further attention.

The soldier then took her workbasket and from it selected bits of silk of various colors, tucked them into his palm, closed his hand upon them, and repeated a prayer, after which he threw the handful into the air. Immediately beautiful butterflies filled the room, dazzling the eyes and shining in all the colors of the silk itself.

The wife, mystified by the wonder of it, forgot her anger. The soldier a little later opened his hand, held it up, and they all flew into it. He closed it tight and then again opened his hand, and they were pieces of silk only. His wife alone saw this; it was unknown to others. No such strange magic was ever heard of before.

In 1637, when Kang-wha fell before the Manchus, all the people of the place fled crying for their lives, while the soldier remained undisturbed at his home, eating his meals with his wife and family just as usual. He laughed at the neighbors hurrying by. Said he, "The barbarians will not touch this town; why do you run so?" Thus it turned out that, while the whole island was devastated, the soldier's village escaped.

CURSED BY THE SNAKE

Ha Yon graduated in the year 1396, and became magistrate of Anak County. He built many pavilions in and about his official place of residence, where people might rest. As he went about his district, seeing the farmers busy, he wrote many songs and verses to encourage them in their work. He became later a royal censor, and King Tai-jong commended him, saying, "Well done, good and faithful servant." Later he became Chief Justice. He cleared out the public offices of all disreputable officials, and made the Court clean. When he had leisure it was his habit to dress in ceremonial garb, burn incense, sit at attention, and write prayer verses the livelong day.

When he was young, once, in the Court of the Crown Prince, he wrote a verse, which was commented upon thus: "Beautiful writing, beautiful thought; truly a treasure." He was a great student and a great inquirer, and grateful and lovable as a friend. He studied as a boy under the patriot Cheung Mong-ju, and was upright and pure in all his ways. His object was to become as one of the Ancients, and so he followed truth, and encouraged men in the study of the sacred books. He used to awake at first cock-crow of the morning, wash, dress, and never lay aside his book. On his right were pictures, on his left were books, and he happy between. He rose to be Prime Minister.

The Story

The old family seat of Prince Ha Yun was in the County of Keum-chon. He was a famous Minister of State in the days of peace and prosperity, and used frequently to find rest and leisure in his summer-house in this same county. It was a large and well-ordered mansion, and was occupied by his children for many years after his death.

The people of that county used to tell a very strange story of Ha and his prosperity, which runs thus: He had placed in an upper room a large crock that was used to hold flour. One day one of the servants, wishing to get some flour from the jar, lifted the lid, when suddenly from the depths of it a huge snake made its appearance. The servant, startled, fell back in great alarm, and then went and told the master what had happened. The master sent his men-slaves and had the jar brought down. They broke it open and let out a huge, awful-looking snake, such as one had never seen before. Several of the servants joined in with clubs and killed the brute. They then piled wood on it and set fire to the whole. Vile fumes arose that filled the house. From the fumes all the people of the place died, leaving no one behind to represent the family. Others who entered the house died also, so that the place became cursed, and was left in desolation. A little later a mysterious fire broke out and burnt up the remaining buildings, leaving only the vacant site. To this day the place is known as "haunted," and no one ventures to build upon it.

THE MAN ON THE ROAD

In the Manchu War of 1636, the people of Seoul rushed off in crowds to make their escape. One party of them came suddenly upon a great force of the enemy, armed and mounted. The hills and valleys seemed full of them, and there was no possible way of escape. What to do they knew not. In the midst of their perplexity they suddenly saw someone sitting peacefully in the main roadway just in front, underneath a pine tree, quite unconcerned. He had dismounted from his horse, which a servant held, standing close by. A screen of several yards of cotton cloth was hanging up just before him, as if to shield him from the dust of the passing army.

The people who were making their escape came up to this stranger, and said imploringly, "We are all doomed to die. What shall we do?"

The mysterious stranger said, "Why should you die? and why are you so frightened? Sit down by me and see the barbarians go by."

The people, perceiving his mind so composed and his of fear, and they having no way of escape, did as he bade them and sat down.

The cavalry of the enemy moved by in great numbers, killing everyone they met, not a single person escaping; but when they reached the place where the magician sat, they went by without, apparently, seeing anything. Thus they continued till the evening, when all had passed by. The stranger and the people with him sat the day through without any harm overtaking them, even though they were in the midst of the enemy's camp, as it were.

At last awaking to the fact that he was possessor of some wonderful magic, they all with one accord came and bowed before him, asking his name and his place of residence. He made no answer, however, but mounted his beautiful horse and rode swiftly away, no one being able to overtake him.

The day following the party fell in with a man who had been captured but had made his escape. They asked if he had seen anything special the day before. He said, "When I followed the barbarian army, passing such and such a point"- indicating the place where the magician had sat with the people- "we skirted great walls and precipitous rocks, against which no one could move, and so we passed by."

Thus were the few yards of cotton cloth metamorphosed before the eyes of the passers-by.

THE OLD MAN WHO BECAME A FISH

Some years ago a noted official became the magistrate of Ko-song County. On a certain day a guest called on him to pay his respects, and when noon came the magistrate had a table of food prepared for him, on which was a dish of skate soup. When the guest saw the soup he twisted his features and refused it, saying, "To-day I am fasting from meat, and so beg to be excused." His face grew very pale, and tears flowed from his eyes. The magistrate thought this behavior strange, and asked him two or three times the meaning of it. When he could no longer withhold a reply, he went into all the particulars and told him the story.

"Your humble servant," he said, "has in his life met with much unheard-of and unhappy experience, which he has never told to a living soul, but now that your Excellency asks it of me, I cannot refrain from telling. Your servant's father was a very old man, nearly a hundred, when one day he was taken down with a high fever, in which his body was like a fiery furnace. Seeing the danger he was in, his children gathered about weeping, thinking

70

that the time of his departure had surely come. But he lived, and a few days later said to us, 'I am burdened with so great a heat in this sickness that I am not able to endure it longer. I would like to go out to the bank of the river that runs before the house and see the water flowing by, and be refreshed by it. Do not disobey me now, but carry me out at once to the water's edge.'

"We remonstrated with him and begged him not to do so, but he grew very angry, and said, 'If you do not as I command, you will be the death of me'; and so, seeing that there was no help for it, we bore him out and placed him on the bank of the river. He, seeing the water, was greatly delighted, and said, 'The clear flowing water cures my sickness.' A moment later he said further, 'I'd like to be quite alone and rid of you all for a little. Go away into the wood and wait till I tell you to come.'

"We again remonstrated about this, but he grew furiously angry, so that we were helpless. We feared that if we insisted, his sickness would grow worse, and so we were compelled to yield. We went a short distance away and then turned to look, when suddenly the old father was gone from the place where he had been seated. We hurried back to see what had happened. My father had taken off his clothes and plunged into the water, which was muddied. His body was already half metamorphosed into a skate. We saw its transformation in terror, and did not dare to go near him, when all at once it became changed into a great flatfish, that swam and plunged and disported itself in the water with intense delight. He looked back at us as though he could hardly bear to go, but a moment later he was off, entered the deep sea, and did not again appear.

"On the edge of the stream where he had changed his form we found his finger-nails and a tooth. These we buried, and to-day as a family we all abstain from skate fish, and when we see the neighbors frying or eating it we are overcome with disgust and horror."

THE GEOMANCER

Yi Eui-sin was a specialist in Geomancy. His craft came into being evidently as a by-product of Taoism, but has had mixed in it elements of ancient Chinese philosophy. The Positive and the Negative, the Two Primary Principles in Nature, play a great part; also the Five Elements, Metal, Wood, Water, Fire and Earth. In the selection of a site, that for a house is called a "male" choice, while the grave is denominated the "female" choice.

Millions of money have been expended in Korea on the geomancer and his associates in the hope of finding lucky homes for the living and auspicious resting-places for the dead, the Korean idea being that, in some mysterious way, all our fortune is associated with Mother Earth.

The Story

There was a geomancer once, Yi Eui-sin, who in seeking out a special mountain vein, started with the Dragon Ridge in North Ham-kyong Province, and traced it as far as Pine Mountain in Yang-ju County, where it stopped in a beautifully rounded end, forming a perfect site for burial. After wandering all day in the hills, Yi's hungry spirit cried out for food. He saw beneath the hill a small house, to which he went, and rapping at the door asked for something to eat. A mourner, recently bereaved, came out in a respectful and kindly way, and gave him a dish of white gruel. Yi, after he had eaten, asked what time the friend had become a mourner, and if he had already passed the funeral. The owner answered, "I am just now entering upon full mourning, but we have not yet arranged for the funeral." He spoke in a sad and disheartened way.

Yi felt sorry for him, and asked the reason. "I wonder if it's because you are poor that you have not yet made the necessary arrangements, or perhaps you have not yet found a suitable site! I am an expert in reading the hills, and I'll tell you of a site; would you care to see it?"

The mourner thanked him most gratefully, and said, "I'll be delighted to know of it."

Yi then showed him the end of the great vein that he had just discovered, also the spot for the grave and how to place its compass points. "After possessing this site," said he, "you will be greatly enriched, but in ten years you will have cause to arrange for another site.

When that comes to pass please call me, won't you? In calling for me just ask for Yi So-pang, who lives in West School Ward, Seoul."

The mourner did as directed, and as the geomancer had foretold, all his affairs prospered. He built a large tiled house, and ornamented the grave with great stones as a prosperous and high-minded country gentleman should do.

After ten years a guest called one day, and saluting him asked, "Is that grave yonder, beyond the stream, yours?" The master answered, "It is mine." Then the stranger said, "That is a famous site, but ten years have passed since you have come into possession of it, and the luck is gone; why do you not make a change? If you wait too long you will rue it and may meet with great disaster."

The owner, hearing this, thought of Yi the geomancer, and what he had said years before. Remembering that, he asked the stranger to remain as his guest while he went next day to Seoul to look up Yi in West School Ward. He found him, and told him why he had come.

Yi said, "I already knew of this." So the two journeyed together to the inquirer's home. When there, they went with the guest up the hill. Yi asked of the guest, "Why did you tell the master to change the site?"

The guest replied, "This hill is a Kneeling Pheasant formation. If the pheasant kneels too long it cannot endure it, so that within a limited time it must fly. Ten years is the time; that's why I spoke."

Yi laughed and said, "Your idea is only a partial view, you have thought of only one thing, there are other conditions that enter." Then he showed the peak to the rear, and said, "Yonder is Dog Hill," and then one below, "which," said he, "is Falcon Hill," and then the stream in front, "which," said he, "is Cat River. This is the whole group, the dog behind, the falcon just above, and the cat in front, how then can the pheasant fly? It dares not."

The guest replied, "Teacher, surely your eyes are enlightened, and see further than those of ordinary men."

From that day forth the Yis of Pine Hill became a great and noted family.

THE MAN WHO BECAME A PIG

Kim Yu was the son of a country magistrate who graduated with literary honors in 1596. In 1623 he was one of the faithful courtiers who joined forces to dethrone the wicked Prince Kwang-hai, and place In-jo on the throne. He was raised to the rank of Prince and became, later, Prime Minister. In the year 1624, when Yi Kwal raised an insurrection, he was the means of putting it down and of bringing many of his followers to justice. In 1648, he died at the age of seventy-seven.

In the last year of Son-jo the King called his grandchildren together and had them write Chinese for him and draw pictures. At that time In-jo was a little boy, and he drew a picture of a horse. King Son-jo gave the picture to Yi Hang-bok, but when the latter some years later went into exile he gave the picture to Kim Yu. Kim Yu took it, and hung it up in his house and there it remained.

Prince In-jo was one day making a journey out of the Palace when he was overtaken by rain, and took refuge in a neighboring gate-quarters. A servant-maid came out and invited him in, asking him not to stand in the wet, but

Prince In-jo declined. The invitation, however, was insisted on, and he went into the guest-room, where he saw the picture of a horse on the wall. On examining it carefully he recognized it as the picture he had drawn when a lad, and he wondered how it could have come here. Kim Yu then came in and they met for the first time. Prince In-jo told him how he had been overtaken by rain and invited in. He asked concerning the picture of the horse that hung on the wall, and Kim Yu in reply asked why he inquired. Prince In-jo said, "I drew that picture myself when I was a boy." Just as they spoke together a rich table of food was brought in from the inner quarters. Kim Yu, not knowing yet who his guest was, looked with wonder at this surprise, and after Prince In-jo had gone, he inquired of his wife why she had sent such delicious fare in to a stranger. The wife replied, "In a dream last night, I saw the King come and stand in front of our house. I was just thinking it over when the servant came in and said that someone was standing before the door. I looked out, and lo, it was the man I had seen in my dream! so I have treated him to the best of hospitality that I was able." Kim Yu soon learned who his caller had been, and became from that time the faithful supporter of Prince In-jo, and later helped to put him on the throne.

After In-jo became king he asked privately of Kim Yu where he had got the picture. Kim Yu said, "I got it from Prince Yi Hang-bok."

Kim Yu then called Yi's son and inquired of him as to how his father had got it. The son said, "In the last year of King Son-jo he called my father along with all his grandchildren, and showed him the writings and drawings of the young princes. My father looked at them with interest, but the King gave him only one as a keepsake, namely, the drawing of the horse." In the picture there was a willow tree and a horse tied to it. Kim Yu then recognized the thought that underlay the gift of the picture, namely, that Prince Yi Hang-bok should support In-jo in the succession to the throne.

The Story

A certain Minister of State, called Kim Yu, living in the County of Seung-pyong, had a relative who resided in a far-distant part of the country, an old man aged nearly one hundred. On a certain day a son of this patriarch came to the office of the Minister and asked to see him. Kim ordered him to be admitted, and inquired as to why he had come. Said he, "I have something very important to say, a private matter to lay before your Excellency. There are so many guests with you now that I'll come again in the evening and tell it."

In the evening, when all had departed, he came, and the Minister ordered out his personal retainers and asked the meaning of the call. The man replied, saying, "My father, though very old, was, as you perhaps know, a strong and hearty man. On a certain day he called us children to him and said, 'I wish to have a siesta, so now close the door and all of you go out of the room. Do not let anyone venture in till I call you.'

"We children agreed, of course, and did so. Till late at night there was neither call nor command to open the door, so that we began to be anxious. We at last looked through the chink, and lo, there was our father changed into a huge pig! Terrified by the sight of it we opened the door and looked in, when the animal grunted and growled and made a rush to get out past us. We hurriedly closed the door again and held a consultation.

"Some said, 'Let's keep the pig just as it is, within doors, and care for it.' Some said, 'Let's have a funeral and bury it.' We ignorant country-folk not knowing just what to do under such peculiar circumstances, I have come to ask counsel of your Excellency. Please think over this startling phenomenon and tell us what we ought to do."

Prince Kim, hearing this, gave a great start, thought it over for a long time, and at last said, "No such mysterious thing was ever heard of before, and I really don't know what is best to do under the circumstances, but still, it seems to me that since this metamorphosis has come about, you had better not bury it before death, so give up the funeral idea. Since, too, it is not a human being any longer, I do not think it right to keep it in the house. You say that it wants to make its escape, and as a cave in the woods or hills is its proper abode, I think you had better take it out and let it go free into the trackless depths of some mountainous country, where no foot of man has ever trod."

The son accepted this wise counsel, and did as the Minister advised, took it away into the deep mountains and let it go. Then he donned sackcloth, mourned, buried his father's clothes for a funeral, and observed the day of metamorphosis as the day of sacrificial ceremony.

THE OLD WOMAN WHO BECAME A GOBLIN

There was a Confucian scholar once who lived in the southern part of Seoul. It is said that he went out for a walk one day while his wife remained alone at home. When he was absent there came by begging an old woman who looked like a Buddhist priestess, for while very old her face was not wrinkled. The scholar's wife asked her if she knew how to sew. She said she did, and so the wife made this proposition, "If you will stay and work for me I'll give you your breakfast and your supper, and you'll not have to beg anywhere; will you agree?"

She replied, "Oh, thank you so much, I'll be delighted."

The scholar's wife, well satisfied with her bargain, took her in and set her to picking cotton, and making and spinning thread. In one day she did more than eight ordinary women, and yet had, seemingly, plenty of time to spare. The wife, delighted above measure, treated her to a great feast. After five or six days, however, the feeling of delight and the desire to treat her liberally and well wore off somewhat, so that the old woman grew angry and said, "I am tired of living alone, and so I want your husband for my partner." This being refused, she went off in a rage, but came back in a little accompanied by a decrepit old man who looked like a Buddhist beggar.

These two came boldly into the room and took possession, cleared out the things that were in the ancient tablet-box on the wall-shelf, and both disappeared into it, so that they were not seen at all, but only their voices heard. According to the whim that took them they now ordered eatables and other things. When the scholar's wife failed in the least particular to please them, they sent plague and sickness after her, so that her children fell sick and died. Relatives on hearing of this came to see, but they also caught the plague, fell ill and died. Little by little no one dared come near the place, and it became known at last that the wife was held as a prisoner by these two goblin creatures. For a time smoke was seen by the town-folk coming out of the chimney daily, and they knew that the wife still lived, but after five or six days the smoke ceased, and they knew then that the woman's end had come. No one dared even to make inquiry.

THE GRATEFUL GHOST

It is often told that in the days of the Koryo Dynasty (A.D. 918–1392), when an examination was to be held, a certain scholar came from a far-distant part of the country to take part. Once on his journey the day was drawing to a close, and he found himself among the mountains. Suddenly he heard a sneezing from among the creepers and bushes by the roadside, but could see no one. Thinking it strange, he dismounted from his horse, went into the brake and listened. He heard it again, and it seemed to come from the roots of the creeper close beside him, so he ordered his servant to dig round it and see. He dug and found a dead man's skull. It was full of earth, and the roots of the creeper had passed through the nostrils. The sneezing was caused by the annoyance felt by the spirit from having the nose so discommoded.

The candidate felt sorry, washed the skull in clean water, wrapped it in paper and reburied it in its former place on the hill-side. He also brought a table of food and offered sacrifice, and said a prayer.

That night, in a dream, a scholar came to him, an old man with white hair, who bowed, thanked him, and said, "On account of sin committed in a former life, I died out of season before I had fulfilled my days. My posterity, too, were all destroyed, my body crumbled back into the dust, my skull alone remaining, and that is what you found below the creeper. On account of the root passing through it the annoyance was great, and I could not help but sneeze. By good luck you and your kind heart, blessed of Heaven, took pity on me, buried me in a clean place and gave me food. Your kindness is greater than the mountains, and like the blessing that first brought me into life. Though my soul is by no means perfect, yet I long for some way by which to requite your favor, and so I have exercised my powers in your behalf. Your present journey is for the purpose of trying the official Examination, so I shall tell you beforehand what the form is to be, and the subject. It is to be of character groups of fives, in couplets; the rhyme sound is 'pong,' and the subject 'Peaks and Spires of the Summer Clouds.' I have already composed one for you, which, if you care to use it, will undoubtedly win you the first place. It is this—

'The white sun rode high up in the heavens,
    And the floating clouds formed a lofty peak;

The priest who saw them asked if there was a temple there,

And the crane lamented the fact that no pines were visible;

But the lightnings from the cloud were the flashings of the woodman's axe,

And the muffled thunders were the bell calls of the holy temple.

Will any say that the hills do not move?

On the sunset breezes they sailed away.'"

After thus stating it, he bowed and took his departure.

The man, in wonder, awakened from his dream, came up to Seoul; and behold, the subject was as foretold by the spirit. He wrote what had been given him, and became first in the honors of the occasion.

THE PLUCKY MAIDEN

Han Myong-hoi.- We are told in the Yol-ryok Keui-sul that when Han was a boy he had for protector and friend a tiger, who used to accompany him as a dog does his master. One evening, when he started off into the hills, he heard the distant tramp of the great beast, who had got scent of his going, and had come rushing after him. When Han saw him he turned, and said, "Good old chap, you come all this distance to be my friend; I love you for it." The tiger prostrated himself and nodded with his head several times. He used to accompany Han all through the nights, but when the day dawned he would leave him.

Han later fell into bad company, grew fond of drink, and was one of the boisterous companions of King Se-jo.

The Story

Han Myong-hoi was a renowned Minister of the Reign of Se-jo (A.D. 1455–1468). The King appreciated and enjoyed him greatly, and there was no one of the Court who could surpass him for influence and royal favor. Confident in his position, Han did as he pleased, wielding absolute power. At that time, like grass before the wind, the world bowed at his coming; no one dared utter a word of remonstrance.

When Han went as governor to Pyong-an Province he did all manner of lawless things. Any one daring to cross his wishes in the least was dealt with by torture and death. The whole Province feared him as they would a tiger.

On a certain day Governor Han, hearing that the Deputy Prefect of Son-chon had a very beautiful daughter, called the Deputy, and said, "I hear that you have a very beautiful daughter, whom I would like to make my concubine. When I am on my official rounds shortly, I shall expect to stop at your town and take her. So be ready for me."

The Deputy, alarmed, said, "How can your Excellency say that your servant's contemptible daughter is beautiful? Someone has reported her wrongly. But since you so command, how can I do but accede gladly?" So he bowed, said his farewell, and went home.

On his return his family noticed that his face was clouded with anxiety, and the daughter asked why it was. "Did the Governor call you, father?" asked she; "and why are you so anxious? Tell me, please." At first, fearing that she would be disturbed, he did not reply, but her repeated questions forced him, so that he said, "I am in trouble on your account," and then told of how the Governor wanted her for his concubine. "If I had refused I would have been killed, so I yielded; but a gentleman's daughter being made a concubine is a disgrace unheard of."

The daughter made light of it and laughed. "Why did you not think it out better than that, father? Why should a grown man lose his life for the sake of a girl? Let the daughter go. By losing one daughter and saving your life, you surely do better than saving your daughter and losing your life. One can easily see where the greater advantage lies. A daughter does not count; give her over, that's all. Don't for a moment think otherwise, just put away your distress and anxiety. We women, every one of us, are under the ban, and such things are decreed by Fate. I shall accept without any opposition, so please have no anxiety. It is settled now, and you, father, must yield and follow. If you do so all will be well."

The father sighed, and said in reply, "Since you seem so willing, my mind is somewhat relieved." But from this time on the whole house was in distress. The girl alone seemed perfectly unmoved, not showing the slightest sign of fear. She laughed as usual, her light and happy laugh, and her actions seemed wonderfully free.

In a little the Governor reached Son-chon on his rounds. He then called the Deputy, and said, "Make ready your daughter for to-morrow and all the things needed." The Deputy came home and made preparation for the so-called wedding. The daughter said, "This is not a real wedding; it is only the taking of a concubine, but still, make everything ready in the way of refreshments and ceremony as for a real marriage." So the father did as she requested.

On the day following the Governor came to the house of the Deputy. He was not dressed in his official robes, but came simply in the dress and hat of a commoner. When he went into the inner quarters he met the daughter; she stood straight before him. Her two hands were lifted in ceremonial form, but instead of holding a fan to hide her face she held a sword before her. She was very pretty. He gave a great start of surprise, and asked the meaning of the knife that she held. She ordered her nurse to reply, who said, "Even though I am an obscure countrywoman, I do not forget that I am born of the gentry; and though your Excellency is a high Minister of

State, still to take me by force is an unheard-of dishonor. If you take me as your real and true wife I'll serve you with all my heart, but if you are determined to take me as a concubine I shall die now by this sword. For that reason I hold it. My life rests on one word from your Excellency. Speak it, please, before I decide."

The Governor, though a man who observed no ceremony and never brooked a question, when he saw how beautiful and how determined this maiden was, fell a victim to her at once, and said, "If you so decide, then, of course, I'll make you my real wife."

Her answer was, "If you truly mean it, then please withdraw and write out the certificate; send the gifts; provide the goose; dress in the proper way; come, and let us go through the required ceremony; drink the pledge-glass, and wed."

The Governor did as she suggested, carried out the forms to the letter, and they were married.

She was not only a very pretty woman, but upright and true of soul- a rare person indeed. The Governor took her home, loved her and held her dear. He had, however, a real wife before and concubines, but he set them all aside and fixed his affections on this one only. She remonstrated with him over his wrongs and unrighteous acts, and he listened and made improvement. The world took note of it, and praised her as a true and wonderful woman. She counted herself the real wife, but the first wife treated her as a concubine, and all the relatives said likewise that she could never be considered a real wife. At that time King Se-jo frequently, in the dress of a commoner, used to visit Han's house. Han entertained him royally with refreshments, which his wife used to bring and offer before him. He called her his "little sister." On a certain day King Se-jo, as he was accustomed, came to the house, and while he was drinking he suddenly saw the woman fall on her face before him. The King in surprise inquired as to what she could possibly mean by such an act. She then told all the story of her being taken by force and brought to Seoul. She wept while she said, "Though I am from a far-distant part of the country I am of the gentry by ancestry, and my husband took me with all the required ceremonies of a wife, so that I ought not to be counted a concubine. But there is no law in this land by which a second real wife may be taken after a first real wife exists, so they call me a concubine, a matter of deepest disgrace. Please, your Majesty, take pity on me and decide my case."

The King laughed, and said, "This is a simple matter to settle; why should my little sister make so great an affair of it, and bow before me? I will decide your case at once. Come." He then wrote out with his own hand a document making her a real wife, and her children eligible for the highest office. He wrote it, signed it, stamped it and gave it to her.

From that time on she was known as a real wife, in rank and standing equal to the first one. No further word was ever slightingly spoken, and her children shared in the affairs of State.

THE RESOURCEFUL WIFE

In the last year of Yon-san terrible evils were abroad among the people. Such wickedness as the world had never seen before was perpetrated, of which his Majesty was the evil genius. He even gave orders to his eunuchs and underlings to bring to him any women of special beauty that they might see in the homes of the highest nobility, and whoever pleased him he used as his own. "Never mind objections," said he, "take them by force and come." Such were his orders. No one escaped him. He even went so far as to publish abroad that Minister So and So's wife preferred him to her husband and would like to live always in the Palace. It was the common talk of the city, and people were dumbfounded.

For that reason all hearts forsook him, and because of this he was dethroned, and King Choong-jong reigned in his stead.

In these days of trouble there was a young wife of a certain minister, who was very beautiful in form and face. One day it fell about that she was ordered into the Palace. Other women, when called, would cry and behave as though their lives were forfeited, but this young woman showed not the slightest sign of fear. She dressed and went straight into the Palace. King Yon-san saw her, and ordered her to come close to him. She came, and then in a sudden manner the most terrible odor imaginable was noticeable. The King held his fan before his face, turned aside, spat, and said, "Dear me, I cannot stand this one, take her away," and so she escaped undefiled.

How it came about was thus: She knew that she was likely to be called at any moment, and so had planned a ruse by which to escape. Two slices of meat she had kept constantly on hand, decayed and foul-smelling, but always ready. She placed these under her arms as she dressed and went into the Palace, and so provided this awful and unaccountable odor.

All that knew of it praised her bravery and sagacity.

THE BOXED-UP GOVERNOR

A certain literary official was at one time Governor of the city of Kyong-ju. Whenever he visited the Mayor of the place, it was his custom, on seeing dancing-girls, to tap them on the head with his pipe, and say, "These girls are devils, ogres, goblins. How can you tolerate them in your presence?"

Naturally, those who heard this disliked him, and the Mayor himself detested his behavior and manners. He sent a secret message to the dancing-girls, saying, "If any of you, by any means whatever, can deceive this governor, and put him to shame, I'll reward you richly." Among them there was one girl, a mere child, who said she could.

The Governor resided in the quarter of the city where the Confucian Temple was, and he had but one servant with him, a young lad. The dancing-girl who had decided to ensnare him, in the dress of a common woman of the town, used frequently to go by the main gateway of the Temple, and in going would call the Governor's boy to her. Sometimes she showed her profile and sometimes she showed her whole form, as she stood in the gateway. The boy would go out to her and she would speak to him for a moment or two and then go. She came sometimes once a day, sometimes twice, and this she kept up for a long time. The Governor at last inquired of the boy as to who this woman was that came so frequently to call him.

"She is my sister," said the boy. "Her husband went away on a peddling round a year or so ago, and has not yet returned; consequently she has no one else to help her, so she frequently calls and confers with me."

One evening, when the boy had gone to eat his meal and the Governor was alone, the woman came to the main gateway, and called for the boy.

His Excellency answered for him, and invited her in. When she came, she blushed, and appeared very diffident, standing modestly aside.

The Governor said, "My boy is absent just now, but I want a smoke; go and get a light for my pipe, will you, please."

She brought the light, and then he said, "Sit down too, and smoke a little, won't you?"

She replied, "How could I dare do such a thing?"

He said, "There is no one else here now; never mind."

There being no help for it, she did as he bade her, and smoked a little. He felt his heart suddenly inclined in her favor, and he said, "I have seen many beautiful women, but I surely think that you are the prettiest of them all. Once seeing you, I have quite forgotten how to eat or sleep. Could you not come to me to live here? I am quite alone and no one will know it."

She pretended to be greatly scandalized. "Your Excellency is a noble, and I am a low-class woman; how can you think of such a thing? Do you mean it as a joke?"

He replied, "I mean it truly, no joke at all." He swore an oath, saying, "Really I mean it, every word."

She then said, "Since you speak so, I am really very grateful, and shall come."

Said he, "Meeting you thus is wonderful indeed."

She went on to say, "There is another matter, however, that I wish to call to your attention. I understand that where your Excellency is now staying is a very sacred place, and that according to ancient law men were forbidden to have women here. Is that true?"

The Governor clapped her shoulder, and said, "Well, really now, how is it that you know of this? You are right. What shall we do about it?"

She made answer, "If you'll depend on me, I'll arrange a plan. My home is nearby, and I am also alone, so if you come quietly at night to me, we can meet and no one will know. I shall send a felt hat by the boy, and you can wear that for disguise. With this commoner's felt hat on no one will know you."

The Governor was greatly delighted, and said, "How is it that you can plan so wonderfully? I shall do as you suggest. Now you be sure to be on hand." He repeated this two or three times.

The woman went and entered the house indicated. When evening came she sent the hat by the boy. The Governor arrived as agreed, and she received him, lit the lamp, and brought him refreshments and drink. They talked and drank together, and he called her to come to him. The woman hesitated for a moment, when suddenly there was a call heard from the outside, and a great disturbance took place. She bent her head to listen and then gave a cry of alarm, saying, "That's the voice of my husband, who has come. I was unfortunate, and so had this miserable wretch apportioned to my lot. He is the most despicable among mortals. For murder and arson he has no equal. Three years ago he left me and I took another husband, and we've had nothing to do with each other since. I can't imagine why he should come now. He is evidently very drunk, too, from the sound of his voice. Your Excellency has really fallen into a terrible plight. What shall I do?"

The woman went out then and answered, saying, "Who comes thus at midnight to make such a disturbance?"

The voice replied, "Don't you know my voice? Why don't you open the door?"

She answered, "Are you not Chol-lo (Brass Tiger), and have we not separated for good, years ago? Why have you come?"

The voice from without answered back, "Your leaving me and taking another man has always been a matter of deepest resentment on my part; I have something special to say to you," and he pounded the door open and came thundering in.

The woman rushed back into the room, saying, "Your Excellency must escape in some way or other."

In such a little thatched hut there was no place possible for concealment but an empty rice-box only. "Please get into this," said she, and she lifted the lid and hurried him in. The Governor, in his haste and déshabille, was bundled into the box. He then heard, from within, this fellow come into the room and quarrel with his wife. She said, "We have been separated three years already; what reason have you to come now and make such a disturbance?"

Said he, "You cast me off and took another man, therefore I have come for the clothes that I left, and the other things that belong to me."

Then she threw out his belongings to him, but he said, pointing to the box, "That's mine."

She replied, "That's not yours; I bought that myself with two rolls of silk goods."

"But," said he, "one of those rolls I gave you, and I'm not going to let you have it."

"Even though you did give it, do you mean to say that for one roll of silk you will carry away this box? I'll not consent to it." Thus they quarreled, and contradicted each other.

"If you don't give me the box," said he, "I'll enter a suit against you at the Mayor's."

A little later the day dawned, and so he had the box carried off to the Mayor's office to have the case decided by law, while the woman followed. When they entered the court, already the Mayor was seated in the judgment-place, and here they presented their case concerning the box.

The Mayor, after hearing, decided thus: "Since you each have a half-share in its purchase, there is nothing for me to do but to divide it between you. Bring a saw," said he.

The servants brought the saw and began on the box, when suddenly from the inner regions came forth a cry, "Save me; oh, save me!"

The Mayor, in pretended astonishment, said, "Why, there's a man's voice from the inside," and ordered that it should be opened. The servants managed to find the key, and at last the lid came back, and from the inner quarters there came forth a half-dressed man.

On seeing him the whole place was put into convulsions of laughter, for it was none other than the Governor.

"How is it that your Excellency finds yourself in this box in this unaccountable way?" asked the Mayor. "Please come out."

The Governor, huddling himself together as well as he could, climbed on to the open verandah. He held his head down and nearly died for shame.

The Mayor, splitting his sides with laughter, ordered clothes to be brought, and the first thing that came was a woman's green dress-coat. The Governor hastily turned it inside out, slipped it on, and made a dash for his quarters in the Confucian Temple. That day he left the place never to return, and even to the present time in Kyong-ju they laugh and tell the story of the Boxed-up Governor.

THE MAN WHO LOST HIS LEGS

There was a merchant in Chong-ju who used to go to Quelpart to buy seaweed. One time when he drew up on the shore he saw a man shuffling along on the ground toward the boat. He crept nearer, and at last took hold of the side with both his hands and jumped in.

"When I looked at him," said the merchant, "I found he was an old man without any legs. Astonished, I asked, saying, 'How is it, old man, that you have lost your legs?'

"He said in reply, 'I lost my legs on a trip once when I was shipwrecked, and a great fish bit them off.'"

"However did that happen?" inquired the merchant. And the old man said, "We were caught in a gale and driven till we touched on some island or other. Before us on the shore stood a high castle with a great gateway. The twenty or so of us who were together in the storm-tossed boat were all exhausted from cold and hunger, and lying exposed. We landed and managed to go together to the house. There was in it one man only, whose height was terrible to behold, and whose chest many spans was round. His face was black and his eyes large and rolling. His voice like the braying of a monster donkey. Our people made motions showing that they wanted something to eat. The man made no reply, but securely fastened the front gate. After this he brought an armful of wood, put it in the middle of the courtyard, and there made a fire. When the fire blazed up he rushed after us and caught a young lad, one of our company, cooked him before our eyes, pulled him to pieces and ate him. We were all reduced to a state of horror, not knowing what to do. We gazed at each other in dismay and stupefaction.

"When he had eaten his fill, he went up into a verandah and opened a jar, from which he drank some kind of spirit. After drinking it he uttered the most gruesome and awful noises; his face grew very red and he lay down and slept. His snoring were like the roarings of the thunder. We planned then to make our escape, and so tried to open the large gate, but one leaf was about twenty-four feet across, and so thick and heavy that with all our strength we could not move it. The walls, too, were a hundred and fifty feet high, and so we could do nothing with them. We were like fish in a pot- beyond all possible way of escape. We held each other's hands, and cried.

"Among us, one man thought of this plan: We had a knife and he took it, and while the monster was drunk and asleep, decided to stab his eyes out, and cut his throat. We said in reply, 'We are all doomed to death, anyway; let's try,' and we made our way up on to the verandah and stabbed his eyes. He gave an awful roar, and struck out on all sides to catch us. We rushed here and there, making our escape out of the court back into the rear garden. There were in this enclosure pigs and sheep, about sixty of them in all. There we rushed, in among the pigs and sheep. He floundered about, waving his two arms after us, but not one of us did he get hold of; we were all mixed up- sheep, pigs and people. When he did catch anything it was a sheep; and when it was not a sheep it was a pig. So he opened the front gate to send all the animals out.

"We then each of us took a pig or sheep on the back and made straight for the gate. The monster felt each, and finding it a pig or a sheep let it go. Thus we all got out and rushed for the boat. A little later he came and sat on the bank and roared his threatening at us. A lot of other giants came at his call. They took steps of thirty feet or so, came racing after us, caught the boat, and made it fast; but we took axes and struck at the hands that held it, and so got free at last and out to the open sea.

"Again a great wind arose, and we ran on to the rocks and were all destroyed. Everyone was engulfed in the sea and drowned; I alone got hold of a piece of boat-timber and lived. Then there was a horrible fish from the sea that came swimming after me and bit off my legs. At last I drifted back home and here I am.

"When I think of it still, my teeth are cold and my bones shiver. My Eight Lucky Stars are very bad, that's why it happened to me."

TEN THOUSAND DEVILS

Han Chun-kyom was the son of a provincial secretary. He matriculated in the year 1579 and graduated in 1586. He received the last wishes of King Son-jo, and sat by his side taking notes for seven hours. From 1608 to 1623 he was generalissimo of the army, and later was raised to the rank of Prince.

A certain Prince Han of Choong-chong Province had a distant relative who was an uncouth countryman living in extreme poverty. This relative came to visit him from time to time. Han pitied his cold and hungry condition, gave him clothes to wear and shared his food, urging him to stay and to prolong his visit often into several months. He felt sorry for him, but disliked his uncouthness and stupidity.

On one of these visits the poor relation suddenly announced his intention to return home, although the New Year's season was just at hand. Han urged him to remain, saying, "It would be better for you to be comfortably housed at my home, eating cake and soup and enjoying quiet sleep rather than riding through wind and weather at this season of the year."

He said at first that he would have to go, until his host so insistently urged on him to stay that at last he yielded and gave consent. At New Year's Eve he remarked to Prince Han, "I am possessor of a peculiar kind of magic, by which I have under my control all manner of evil genii, and New Year is the season at which I call them up, run over their names, and inspect them. If I did not do so I should lose control altogether, and there would follow no end of trouble among mortals. It is a matter of no small moment, and that is why I wished to go. Since, however, you have detained me, I shall have to call them up in your Excellency's house and look them over. I hope you will not object."

Han was greatly astonished and alarmed, but gave his consent. The poor relation went on to say further, "This is an extremely important matter, and I would like to have for it your central guest hall."

Han consented to this also, so that night they washed the floors and scoured them clean. The relation also sat himself with all dignity facing the south, while Prince Han took up his station on the outside prepared to spy. Soon he saw a startling variety of demons crushing in at the door, horrible in appearance and awesome of manner. They lined up one after another, and still another, and another, till they filled the entire court, each bowing as he came before the master, who, at this point, drew out a book, opened it before him, and began calling off the names. Demon guards who stood by the threshold repeated the call and checked off the names just as they do in a government yamen. From the second watch it went on till the fifth of the morning. Han remarked, "It was indeed no lie when he told me 'ten thousand devils.'"

One late-comer arrived after the marking was over, and still another came climbing over the wall. The man ordered them to be arrested, and inquiry made of them under the paddle. The late arrival said, "I really have had a hard time of it of late to live, and so was obliged, in order to find anything, to inject smallpox into the home of a scholar who lives in Yong-nam. It is a long way off, and so I have arrived too late for the roll-call, a serious fault indeed, I confess."

The one who climbed the wall, said, "I, too, have known want and hunger, and so had to insert a little typhus into the family of a gentleman who lives in Kyong-keui, but hearing that roll-call was due I came helter-skelter, fearing lest I should arrive too late, and so climbed the wall, which was indeed a sin."

The man then, in a loud voice, rated them soundly, saying, "These devils have disobeyed my orders, caused disease and sinned grievously. Worse than everything, they have climbed the wall of a high official's house." He ordered a hundred blows to be given them with the paddle, the cangue to be put on, and to have them locked fast in prison. Then, calling the others to him, he said, "Do not spread disease! Do you understand?" Three times he ordered it and five times he repeated it. Then they were all dismissed. The crowd of devils lined off before him, taking their departure and crushing out through the gate with no end of noise and confusion. After a long time they had all disappeared.

Prince Han, looking on during this time, saw the man now seated alone in the hall. It was quiet, and all had vanished. The cocks crew and morning came. Han was astonished above measure, and asked as to the law that governed such work as this. The poor relation said in reply, "When I was young I studied in a monastery in the mountains. In that monastery was an old priest who had a most peculiar countenance. A man feeble and ready to die, he seemed. All the priests made sport of him and treated him with contempt. I alone had pity on his age, and often gave him of my food and always treated him kindly. One evening, when the moon was bright, the old priest said to me, 'There is a cave behind this monastery from which a beautiful view may be had; will you not come with me and share it?'

"I went with him, and when we crossed the ridge of the hills into the stillness of the night he drew a book from his breast and gave it to me, saying, 'I, who am old and ready to die, have here a great secret, which I have long wished to pass on to someone worthy. I have travelled over the wide length of Korea, and have never found the man till now I meet you, and my heart is satisfied, so please receive it.'

"I opened the book and found it a catalogue list of devils, with magic writing interspersed, and an explanation of the laws that govern the spirit world. The old priest wrote out one magic recipe, and having set fire to it countless devils at once assembled, at which I was greatly alarmed. He then sat with me and called over the names one after the other, and said to the devils, 'I am an old man now, am going away, and so am about to put you under the care of this young man; obey him and all will be well.'

"I already had the book, and so called them to me, read out the new orders, and dismissed them.

"The old priest and I returned to the Temple and went to sleep. I awoke early next morning and went to call on him, but he was gone. Thus I came into possession of the magic art, and have possessed it for a score of years and more. What the world knows nothing of I have thus made known to your Excellency."

Han was astonished beyond measure, and asked, "May I not also come into possession of this wonderful gift?"

The man replied, "Your Excellency has great ability, and can do wonderful things; but the possessor of this craft must be one poor and despised, and of no account. For you, a minister, it would never do."

The next day he left suddenly, and returned no more. Han sent a servant with a message to him. The servant, with great difficulty, at last found him alone among a thousand mountain peaks, living in a little straw hut no bigger than a cockle shell. No neighbors were there, nor any one beside. He called him, but he refused to come. He sent another messenger to invite him, but he had moved away and no trace of him was left.

Prince Han's children had heard this story from himself, and I, the writer, received it from them.

THE HOME OF THE FAIRIES

In the days of King In-jo (1623–1649) there was a student of Confucius who lived in Ka-pyong. He was still a young man and unmarried. His education had not been extensive, for he had read only a little in the way of history and literature. For some reason or other he left his home and went into Kang-won Province. Travelling on horseback, and with a servant, he reached a mountain, where he was overtaken by rain that wet him through. Mysteriously, from some unknown cause, his servant suddenly died, and the man, in fear and distress, drew the body to the side of the hill, where he left it and went on his way weeping. When he had gone but a short distance, the horse he rode fell under him and died also. Such was his plight: his servant dead, his horse dead, rain falling fast, and the road an unknown one. He did not know what to do or where to go, and reduced thus to walking, he broke down and cried. At this point there met him an old man with very wonderful eyes, and hair as white as snow. He asked the young man why he wept, and the reply was that his servant was dead, his horse was dead, that it was raining, and that he did not know the way. The patriarch, on hearing this, took pity on him, and lifting his staff, pointed, saying, "There is a house yonder, just beyond those pines, follow that stream and it will bring you to where there are people."

The young man looked as directed, and a li or so beyond he saw a clump of trees. He bowed, thanked the stranger, and started on his way. When he had gone a few paces he looked back, but the friend had disappeared. Greatly wondering, he went on toward the place indicated, and as he drew near he saw a grove of pines, huge trees they were, a whole forest of them. Bamboos appeared, too, in countless numbers, with a wide stream of water flowing by. Underneath the water there seemed to be a marble flooring like a great pavement, white and pure. As he went along he saw that the water was all of an even depth, such as one could cross easily. A mile or so farther on he saw a beautifully decorated house. The pillars and entrance approaches were perfect in form. He continued his way, wet as he was, carrying his thorn staff, and entered the gate and sat down to rest. It was paved, too, with marble, and smooth as polished glass. There were no chinks or creases in it, all was of one perfect surface. In the room was a marble table, and on it a copy of the Book of Changes; there was also a brazier of jade just in front. Incense was burning in it, and the fragrance filled the room. Beside these, nothing else was visible. The rain had ceased and all was quiet and clear, with no wind nor anything to disturb. The world of confusion seemed to have receded from him.

While he sat there, looking in astonishment, he suddenly heard the sound of footfalls from the rear of the building. Startled by it, he turned to see, when an old man appeared. He looked as though he might equal the turtle or the crane as to age, and was very dignified. He wore a green dress and carried a jade staff of nine sections. The appearance of the old man was such as to stun any inhabitant of the earth. He recognized him as the master of the place, and so he went forward and made a low obeisance.

The old man received him kindly, and said, "I am the master and have long waited for you." He took him by the hand and led him away. As they went along, the hills grew more and more enchanting, while the soft breezes and the light touched him with mystifying favor. Suddenly, as he looked the man was gone, so he went on by himself, and arrived soon at another palace built likewise of precious stones. It was a great hall, stretching on into the distance as far as the eye could see.

The young man had seen the Royal Palace frequently when in Seoul attending examinations, but compared with this, the Royal Palace was as a mud hut thatched with straw.

As he reached the gate a man in ceremonial robes received him and led him in. He passed two or three pavilions, and at last reached a special one and went up to the upper storey. There, reclining at a table, he saw the ancient sage whom he had met before. Again he bowed.

This young man, brought up poorly in the country, was never accustomed to seeing or dealing with the great. In fear, he did not dare to lift his eyes. The ancient master, however, again welcomed him and asked him to be seated, saying, "This is not the dusty world that you are accustomed to, but the abode of the genii. I knew you were coming, and so was waiting to receive you." He turned and called, saying, "Bring something for the guest to eat."

In a little a servant brought a richly laden table. It was such fare as was never seen on earth, and there was abundance of it. The young man, hungry as he was, ate heartily of these strange viands. Then the dishes were carried away and the old man said, "I have a daughter who has arrived at a marriageable age, and I have been trying to find a son-in-law, but as yet have not succeeded. Your coming accords with this need. Live here, then, and become my son-in-law." The young man, not knowing what to think, bowed and was silent. Then the host turned and gave an order, saying, "Call in the children."

Two boys about twelve or thirteen years of age came running in and sat down beside him. Their faces were so beautifully white they seemed like jewels. The master pointed to them and said to the guest, "These are my sons," and to the sons he said, "This young man is he whom I have chosen for my son-in-law; when should we have the wedding? Choose you a lucky day and let me know."

The two boys reckoned over the days on their fingers, and then together said, "The day after to-morrow is a lucky day."

The old man, turning to the stranger, said, "That decides as to the wedding, and now you must wait in the guest-chamber till the time arrives." He then gave a command to call So and So. In a little an official of the genii came forward, dressed in light and airy garments.

His appearance and expression were very beautiful, a man, he seemed, of glad and happy mien.

The master said, "Show this young man the way to his apartments and treat him well till the time of the wedding."

The official then led the way, and the young man bowed as he left the room. When he had passed outside the gate, a red sedan chair was in waiting for him. He was asked to mount. Eight bearers bore him smoothly along. A mile or so distant they reached another palace, equally wonderful, with no speck or flaw of any kind to mar its beauty. In graceful groves of flowers and trees he descended to enter his pavilion. Beautiful garments were taken from jeweled boxes, and a perfumed bath was given him and a change made. Thus he laid aside his weather-beaten clothes and donned the vestments of the genii. The official remained as company for him till the appointed time.

When that day arrived other beautiful robes were brought, and again he bathed and changed. When he was dressed, he mounted the palanquin and rode to the Palace of the master, twenty or more officials accompanying. On arrival, a guide directed them to the special Palace Beautiful. Here he saw preparations for the wedding, and here he made his bow. This finished he moved as directed, further in. The tinkling sound of jade bells and the breath of sweet perfumes filled the air. Thus he made his entry into the inner quarters.

Many beautiful women were in waiting, all gorgeously appareled, like the women of the gods. Among these he imagined that he would meet the master's daughter. In a little, accompanied by a host of others, she came, shining in jewels and beautiful clothing so that she lighted up the Palace. He took his stand before her, though her face was hidden from him by a fan of pearls. When he saw her at last, so beautiful was she that his eyes were dazzled. The other women, compared with her, were as the magpie to the phœnix. So bewildered was he that he dared not look up. The friend accompanying assisted him to bow and to go through the necessary forms. The ceremony was much the same as that observed among men. When it was over the young man went back to his bridegroom's chamber. There the embroidered curtains, the golden screens, the silken clothing, the jeweled floor, were such as no men of earth ever see.

On the second day his mother-in-law called him to her. Her age would be about thirty, and her face was like a freshly-blown lotus flower. Here a great feast was spread, with many guests invited. The accompaniments thereof in the way of music were sweeter than mortals ever dreamed of. When the feast was over, the women caught up their skirts, and, lifting their sleeves, danced together and sang in sweet accord. The sound of their singing caused even the clouds to stop and listen. When the day was over, and all had well dined, the feast broke up.

A young man, brought up in a country hut, had all of a sudden met the chief of the genii, and had become a sharer in his glory and the accompaniments of his life. His mind was dazed and his thoughts overcame him. Doubts were mixed with fears. He knew not what to do.

A sharer in the joys of the fairies he had actually become, and a year or so passed in such delight as no words can ever describe.

One day his wife said to him, "Would you like to enter into the inner enclosure and see as the fairies see?"

He replied, "Gladly would I."

She then led him into a special park where there were lovely walks, surrounded by green hills. As they advanced there were charming views, with springs of water and sparkling cascades. The scene grew gradually more entrancing, with jeweled flowers and scintillating spray, lovely birds and animals disporting themselves. A man once entering here would never again think of earth as a place to return to.

After seeing this he ascended the highest peak of all, which was like a tower of many stories. Before him lay a wide stretch of sea, with islands of the blessed standing out of the water, and long stretches of pleasant land in view. His wife showed them all to him, pointing out this and that. They seemed filled with golden palaces and surrounded with a halo of light. They were peopled with happy souls, some riding on cranes, some on the phœnix, some on the unicorn; some were sitting on the clouds, some sailing by on the wind, some walking on the air, some gliding gently up the streams, some descending from above, some ascending, some moving west, some north, some gathering in groups. Flutes and harps sounded sweetly. So many and so startling were the things seen that he could never tell the tale of them. After the day had passed they returned.

Thus was their joy unbroken, and when two years had gone by she bore him two sons.

Time moved on, when one day, unexpectedly, as he was seated with his wife, he began to cry and tears soiled his face. She asked in amazement for the cause of it. "I was thinking," said he, "of how a plain countryman living in poverty had thus become the son-in-law of the king of the genii. But in my home is my poor old mother, whom I have not seen for these years; I would so like to see her that my tears flow."

The wife laughed, and said, "Would you really like to see her? Then go, but do not cry." She told her father that her husband would like to go and see his mother. The master called him and gave his permission. The son thought, of course, that he would call many servants and send him in state, but not so. His wife gave him one little bundle and that was all, so he said good-bye to his father-in-law, whose parting word was, "Go now and see your mother, and in a little I shall call for you again."

He sent with him one servant, and so he passed out through the main gateway. There he saw a poor thin horse with a worn rag of a saddle on his back. He looked carefully and found that they were the dead horse and the dead servant, whom he had lost, restored to him. He gave a start, and asked, "How did you come here?"

The servant answered, "I was coming with you on the road when someone caught me away and brought me here. I did not know the reason, but I have been here for a long time."

The man, in great fear, fastened on his bundle and started on his journey. The genie servant brought up the rear, but after a short distance the world of wonder had become transformed into the old weary world again. Here it was with its fogs, and thorn, and precipice. He looked off toward the world of the genii, and it was but a dream. So overcome was he by his feelings that he broke down and cried.

The genie servant said to him when he saw him weeping, "You have been for several years in the abode of the immortals, but you have not yet attained thereto, for you have not yet forgotten the seven things of earth: anger, sorrow, fear, ambition, hate and selfishness. If you once get rid of these there will be no tears for you." On hearing this he stopped his crying, wiped his cheeks, and asked pardon.

When he had gone a mile farther he found himself on the main road. The servant said to him, "You know the way from this point on, so I shall go back," and thus at last the young man reached his home.

He found there an exorcising ceremony in progress. Witches and spirit worshippers had been called and were saying their prayers. The family, seeing the young man come home thus, were all aghast. "It is his ghost," said they. However, they saw in a little that it was really he himself. The mother asked why he had not come home in all that time. She being a very violent woman in disposition, he did not dare to tell her the truth, so he made up something else. The day of his return was the anniversary of his supposed death, and so they had called the witches for a prayer ceremony. Here he opened the bundle that his wife had given him and found four suits of clothes, one for each season.

In about a year after his return home the mother, seeing him alone, made application for the daughter of one of the village literati. The man, being timid by nature and afraid of offending his mother, did not dare to refuse, and was therefore married; but there was no joy in it, and the two never looked at each other.

The young man had a friend whom he had known intimately from childhood. After his return the friend came to see him frequently, and they used to spend the nights talking together. In their talks the friend inquired why in all these years he had never come home. The young man then told him what had befallen him in the land of the genii, and how he had been there and had been married. The friend looked at him in wonder, for he seemed just as he had remembered him except in the matter of clothing. This he found on examination was of very strange material, neither grass cloth, silk nor cotton, but different from them all, and yet warm and comfortable. When spring came the spring clothes sufficed, when summer came those for summer, and for autumn and winter each special suit. They were never washed, and yet never became soiled; they never wore out, and always looked fresh and new. The friend was greatly astonished.

Some three years passed when one day there came once more a servant from the master of the genii, bringing his two sons. There were also letters, saying, "Next year the place where you dwell will be destroyed and all the people will become 'fish and meat' for the enemy, therefore follow this messenger and come, all of you."

He told his friend of this and showed him his two sons. The friend, when he saw these children that looked like silk and jade, confessed the matter to the mother also. She, too, gladly agreed, and so they sold out and had a great feast for all the people of the town, and then bade farewell. This was the year 1635. They left and were never heard of again.

The year following was the Manchu invasion, when the village where the young man had lived was all destroyed. To this day young and old in Ka-pyong tell this story.

THE HONEST WITCH

Song Sang-in matriculated in 1601. He was a just man, and feared by the dishonest element of the Court. In 1605 he graduated and became a provincial governor. He nearly lost his life in the disturbances of the reign of King Kwang-hai, and was exiled to Quelpart for a period of ten years, but in the spring of 1623 he was recalled.

The Story

There was a Korean once, called Song Sang-in, whose mind was upright and whose spirit was true. He hated witches with all his might, and regarded them as deceivers of the people. "By their so-called prayers," said he, "they devour the people's goods. There is no limit to the foolishness and extravagance that accompanies them. This doctrine of theirs is all nonsense. Would that I could rid the earth of them and wipe out their names forever."

Sometime later Song was appointed magistrate of Nam Won County in Chulla Province. On his arrival he issued the following order: "If any witch is found in this county, let her be beaten to death." The whole place was so thoroughly spied upon that all the witches made their escape to other prefectures. The magistrate thought, "Now we are rid of them, and that ends the matter for this county at any rate."

On a certain day he went out for a walk, and rested for a time at Kwang-han Pavilion. As he looked out from his coign of vantage, he saw a woman approaching on horseback with a witch's drum on her head. He looked intently to make sure, and to his astonishment he saw that she was indeed a mutang (witch). He sent a yamen-runner to have her arrested, and when she was brought before him he asked, "Are you a mutang?"

She replied, "Yes, I am."

"Then," said he, "you did not know of the official order issued?"

"Oh yes, I heard of it," was her reply.

He then asked, "Are you not afraid to die, that you stay here in this county?"

The mutang bowed, and made answer, "I have a matter of complaint to lay before your Excellency to be put right; please take note of it and grant my request. It is this: There are true mutangs and false mutangs.

False mutangs ought to be killed, but you would not kill an honest mutang, would you? Your orders pertain to false mutangs; I do not understand them as pertaining to those who are true. I am an honest mutang; I knew you would not kill me, so I remained here in peace."

The magistrate asked, "How do you know that there are honest mutangs?"

The woman replied, "Let's put the matter to the test and see. If I am not proven honest, let me die."

"Very well," said the magistrate; "but can you really make good, and do you truly know how to call back departed spirits?"

The mutang answered, "I can."

The magistrate suddenly thought of an intimate friend who had been dead for some time, and he said to her, "I had a friend of such and such rank in Seoul; can you call his spirit back to me?"

The mutang replied, "Let me do so; but first you must prepare food, with wine, and serve it properly."

The magistrate thought for a moment, and then said to himself, "It is a serious matter to take a person's life; let me find out first if she is true or not, and then decide." So he had the food brought.

The mutang said also, "I want a suit of your clothes, too, please." This was brought, and she spread her mat in the courtyard, placed the food in order, donned the dress, and so made all preliminary arrangements. She then lifted her eyes toward heaven and uttered the strange magic sounds by which spirits are called, meanwhile shaking a tinkling bell. In a little she turned and said, "I've come." Then she began telling the sad story of his sickness and death and their separation. She reminded the magistrate of how they had played together, and of things that had happened when they were at school at their lessons; of the difficulties they had met in the examinations; of experiences that had come to them during their terms of office. She told secrets that they had confided to each other as intimate friends, and many matters most definitely that only they two knew. Not a single mistake did she make, but told the truth in every detail.

The magistrate, when he heard these things, began to cry, saying, "The soul of my friend is really present; I can no longer doubt or deny it." Then he ordered the choicest fare possible to be prepared as a sacrifice to his friend. In a little the friend bade him farewell and took his departure.

The magistrate said, "Alas! I thought mutangs were a brood of liars, but now I know that there are true mutangs as well as false." He gave her rich rewards, sent her away in safety, recalled his order against witches, and refrained from any matters pertaining to them for ever after.

WHOM THE KING HONOURS

In the days of King Se-jong students of the Confucian College were having a picnic to celebrate the Spring Festival. They met in a wood to the north of the college, near a beautiful spring of water, and were drinking and feasting the night through. While they were thus enjoying themselves the rooms of the college were left deserted. One student from the country, a backwoodsman in his way, who was of no account to others, thought that while the rest went away to enjoy themselves someone ought to stay behind to guard the sacred precincts of the temple; so he decided that he would forgo the pleasures of the picnic, stay behind and watch.

The King at that time sent a eunuch to the college to see how many of the students had remained on guard. The eunuch returned, saying that all had gone off on the picnic, except one man, a raw countryman, who was in sole charge. The King at once sent for the man, asking him to come just as he was in his common clothes.

On his arrival his Majesty asked, "When all have gone off for a gay time, why is it that you remain alone?"

He replied, "I, too, would like to have gone, but to leave the sacred temple wholly deserted did not seem to me right, so I stayed."

The King was greatly pleased with this reply, and asked again, "Do you know how to write verses?"

The reply was, "I know only very little about it."

The King then said, "I have one-half of a verse here which runs thus-

'After the rains the mountains weep.'

You write me a mate for this line to go with it."

At once the student replied-

"Before the wind the grass is tipsy."

The King, delighted, praised him for his skill and made him a special graduate on the spot, gave him his diploma, flowers for his hat, and issued a proclamation saying that he had passed the Al-song Examination. At once he ordered for him the head-gear, the red coat, a horse to ride on, two boys to go before, flute-players and harpers, saying, "Go now to the picnic-party and show yourself."

While the picnickers were thus engaged, suddenly they heard the sound of flutes and harps, and they questioned as to what it could mean. This was not the time for new graduates to go abroad. While they looked, behold, here came a victorious candidate, dressed in ceremonial robes, heralded by boys, and riding on the King's palfrey, to greet them. On closer view they saw that it was the uncouth countryman whom they had left behind at the Temple. They asked what it meant, and then learned, to their amazement, that the King had so honored him. The company, in consternation and surprise, broke up and returned home at once.

This special graduate became later, through the favor of the King, a great and noted man.

THE FORTUNES OF YOO

There was a man of Yong-nam, named Yoo, who lived in the days of Se-jong. He had studied the classics, had passed his examinations, and had become a petty official attached to the Confucian College. He was not even of the sixth degree, so that promotion was out of the question. He was a countryman who had no friends and no influence, and though he had long been in Seoul there was no likelihood of any advancement. Such being the case, disheartened and lonely, he decided to leave the city and go back to his country home.

There was a palace secretary who knew this countryman, and who went to say good-bye to him before he left.

Taking advantage of the opportunity, the countryman said, "I have long been in Seoul, but have never yet seen the royal office of the secretaries. Might I accompany you some day when you take your turn?"

The secretary said, "In the daytime there is always a crowd of people who gather there for business, and no one is allowed in without a special pass. I am going in to-morrow, however, and intend to sleep there, so that in the evening we could have a good chance to look the Palace over. People are not allowed to sleep in the Palace as a rule, but doing so once would not be specially noticed." The secretary then gave orders to the military guard who accompanied him to escort this man in the next day.

As the secretary had arranged, the countryman, on the evening following, made his way into the Palace enclosure, but what was his surprise to find that, for some reason or other, the secretary had not come. The gates, also, were closed behind him, so that he could not get out. Really he was in a fix. There chanced to be a body-servant of the secretary in the room, and he, feeling sorry for the stranger, arranged a hidden corner where he might pass the night, and then quietly take his departure in the morning.

The night was beautifully clear, and apparently every one slept but Yoo. He was wide awake, and wondering to himself if he might not go quietly out and see the place.

It was the time of the rainy season, and a portion of the wall had fallen from the enclosure just in front. So Yoo climbed over this broken wall, and, not knowing where he went, found himself suddenly in the royal quarters. It was a beautiful park, with trees, and lakes, and walks. "Whose house is this," thought Yoo, "with its beautiful garden?" Suddenly a man appeared, with a nice new cap on his head, carrying a staff in his hand, and accompanied by a servant, walking slowly towards him. It was no other than King Sejong, taking a stroll in the moonlight with one of his eunuchs.

When they met Yoo had no idea that it was the King. His Majesty asked, "Who are you, and how did you get in here?"

He told who he was, and how he had agreed to come in with the secretary; how the secretary had failed; how the gates were shut and he was a prisoner for the night; how he had seen the bright moonlight and wished to walk out, and, finding the broken wall, had come over. "Whose house is this, anyway?" asked Yoo.

The King replied, "I am the master of this house." His Majesty then asked him in, and made him sit down on a mat beside him. So they talked and chatted together. The King learned that he had passed special examinations in the classics, and inquiring how it was that Yoo had had no better office, Yoo replied that he was an unknown countryman, that his family had no influence, and that, while he desired office, he was forestalled by the powerful families of the capital. "Who is there," he asked, "that would bother himself about me? Thus all my hopes have failed, and I have just decided to leave the city and go back home and live out my days there."

The King asked again, "You know the classics so well, do you know something also of the Book of Changes?"

He replied, "The deeper parts I do not know, but the easier parts only."

Then the King ordered a eunuch to bring the Book of Changes. It was the time when his Majesty was reading it for himself. The book was brought and opened in the moonlight. The King looked up a part that had given him special difficulty, and this the stranger explained character by character, giving the meaning with convincing clearness. The King was delighted and wondered greatly, and so they read together all through the night. When they separated the King said, "You have all this knowledge and yet have never been made use of? Alas, for my country!" said he, sighing.

Yoo remarked that he would like to go straight home now, if the master would kindly open the door for him.

The King said, however, that it was too early yet, and that he might be arrested by the guards who were about. "Go then," said he, "to where you were, and when it is broad daylight you can go through the open gate."

Yoo then bade good-bye, and went back over the broken wall to his corner in the secretary's room. When morning came he went out through the main gateway and returned to his home.

On the following day the King sent a special secretary and had Yoo appointed to the office of Overseer of Literature. On the promulgation of this the officials gathered in the public court, and protested in high dudgeon against so great an office being given to an unknown person.

His Majesty, however, said, "If you are so opposed to it, I'll desist."

But the day following he appointed him to an office one degree still higher. Again they all protested, and his Majesty said, "Really, if you so object, I'll drop the matter."

The day following he appointed him to an office still one degree higher. Again they all protested and he apparently yielded to them. But the day following higher still he was promoted, and again the protests poured in, so much so that his Majesty seemed to yield. On the day following this the King wrote out for him the office of Vice-President of all the Literati.

The high officials gathered again and inquired of one another as to what the King meant, and what they had better do about it. "If we do not in some way prevent it, he will appoint him as President of the Literati." They decided to drop the matter for the present, and see later what was best to do.

A royal banquet was announced to take place, when all the officials gathered. On this occasion the high Ministers of State said quietly to the King, "It is not fitting that so obscure a person have so important an office. Your Majesty's promoting him as you have done has thrown the whole official body into a state of consternation. On our protest you have merely promoted him more. What is your Majesty's reason, please, for this action?"

The King made no reply, but ordered a eunuch to bring the Book of Changes. He opened it at the place of special difficulty, and inquired as to its meaning. Even among the highest ministers not one could give an answer. He inquired by name of this one and that, but all were silent. The King then said, "I am greatly interested in the reading of the Book of Changes; it is the great book of the sages. Anyone who understands it surely ought to be promoted. You, all of you, fail to grasp its meaning, while Yoo, whom you protest against, has explained it all to me. Now what have you to say? Yoo's being promoted thus is just as it ought to be. Why do you object? I shall promote him still more and more, so cease from all opposition."

They were afraid and ashamed, and did not again mention it.

Yoo from that time on became the royal teacher of the Choo-yuk (Book of Changes), and rose higher and higher in rank, till he became Head of the Confucian College and first in influence, surpassing all.

Note.- Many people of ability have no chance for promotion. It is difficult to have one's gifts known in high places; how much more difficult before a king? The good fortune that fell to the first scholar was of God's appointment. By caring for a vacant house the honor came to him, and he was promoted. The other's going thus unbidden into the Palace was a great wrong, but by royal favor he was pardoned, received and honored.

By one line of poetry a man's ability was made manifest, and by one explanation of the Choo-yuk another's path was opened to high promotion.

If Se-jong had not been a great and enlightened king, how could it have happened? Very rare are such happenings, indeed! So all men wondered over what had befallen these two. I, however, wondered more over the King's sagacity in finding them. To my day his virtue and accomplishments are known, so that the world calls him Korea's King of the Golden Age.

AN ENCOUNTER WITH A
HOBGOBLIN

I got myself into trouble in the year Pyong-sin, and was locked up; a military man by the name of Choi Won-so, who was captain of the guard, was involved in it and locked up as well. We often met in prison and whiled away the hours talking together. On a certain day the talk turned on goblins, when Captain Choi said, "When I was young I met with a hobgoblin, which, by the fraction of a hair, almost cost me my life. A strange case indeed!"

I asked him to tell me of it, when he replied, "I had originally no home in Seoul, but hearing of a vacant place in Belt Town, I made application and got it. We went there, my father and the rest of the family occupying the inner quarters, while I lived in the front room.

"One night, late, when I was half asleep, the door suddenly opened, and a woman came in and stood just before the lamp. I saw her clearly, and knew that she was from the home of a scholar friend, for I had seen her before and had been greatly attracted by her beauty, but had never had a chance to meet her. Now, seeing her enter the room thus, I greeted her gladly, but she made no reply. I arose to take her by the hand, when she began walking backwards, so that my hand never reached her. I rushed towards her, but she hastened her backward pace, so that she eluded me. We reached the gate, which she opened with a rear kick, and I followed on after, till she suddenly disappeared. I searched on all sides, but not a trace was there of her. I thought she had merely hidden herself, and never dreamed of anything else.

"On the next night she came again and stood before the lamp just as she had done the night previous. I got up and again tried to take hold of her, but again she began her peculiar pace backwards, till she passed out at the gate and disappeared just as she had done the day before. I was once more surprised and disappointed, but did not think of her being a hobgoblin.

"A few days later, at night, I had lain down, when suddenly there was a sound of crackling paper overhead from above the ceiling. A forbidding, creepy sound it seemed in the midnight. A moment later a curtain was let down that divided the room into two parts. Again, later, a large fire of coals descended right in front of me, while an immense heat filled the place. Where I was seemed all on fire, with no way of escape possible. In terror for my life, I knew not what to do. On the first cock-crow of morning the noise ceased, the curtain went up, and the fire of coals was gone. The place was as though swept with a broom, so clean from every trace of what had happened.

"The following night I was again alone, but had not yet undressed or lain down, when a great stout man suddenly opened the door and came in. He had on his head a soldier's felt hat, and on his body a blue tunic like one of the underlings of the yamen. He took hold of me and tried to drag me out. I was then young and vigorous, and had no intention of yielding to him, so we entered on a tussle. The moon was bright and the night clear, but I, unable to hold my own, was pulled out into the court. He lifted me up and swung me round and round, then went up to the highest terrace and threw me down, so that I was terribly stunned. He stood in front of me and kept me a prisoner. There was a garden to the rear of the house, and a wall round it. I looked, and within the wall were a dozen or so of people. They were all dressed in military hats and coats, and they kept shouting out, 'Don't hurt him, don't hurt him.'

"'The man that mishandled me, however, said in reply, 'It's none of your business, none of your business'; but they still kept up the cry, 'Don't hurt him, don't hurt him'; and he, on the other hand, cried, 'Never you mind; none of your business.' They shouted, 'The man is a gentleman of the military class; do not hurt him.'

"'The fellow merely said in reply, 'Even though he is, it's none of your businesses; so he took me by the two hands and flung me up into the air, till I went half-way and more to heaven. Then in my fall I went shooting past Kyong-keui Province, past Choong-chong, and at last fell to the ground in Chulla. In my flight through space I saw all the county towns of the three provinces as clear as day. Again in Chulla he tossed me up once more. Again I went shooting up into the sky and falling northward, till I found myself at home, lying stupefied below the verandah terrace. Once more I could hear the voices of the group in the garden shouting, 'Don't hurt him- hurt him.' But the man said, 'None of your business- your business.'

"He took me up once more and flung me up again, and away I went speeding off to Chulla, and back I came again, two or three times in all.

"Then one of the group in the garden came forward, took my tormentor by the hand and led him away. They all met for a little to talk and laugh over the matter, and then scattered and were gone, so that they were not seen again.

"I lay motionless at the foot of the terrace till the following morning, when my father found me and had me taken in hand and cared for, so that I came to, and we all left the haunted house, never to go back."

Note.- There are various reasons by which a place may be denominated a "haunted house." The fact that there are hobgoblins in it makes it haunted. If a good or "superior man" enters such a place the goblins move away, and no word of being haunted will be heard. Choi saw the goblin and was greatly injured.

I understand that it is not only a question of men fearing the goblins, but they also fear men. The fact that there are so few people that they fear is the saddest case of all. Choi was afraid of the goblins, that is why they troubled him.

THE SNAKE'S REVENGE

There lived in ancient days an archer, whose home was near the Water Gate of Seoul. He was a man of great strength and famous for his valour.

Water Gate has reference to a hole under the city wall, by which the waters of the Grand Canal find their exit. In it are iron pickets to prevent people's entering or departing by that way.

On a certain afternoon when this military officer was taking a walk, a great snake was seen making its way by means of the Water Gate. The snake's head had already passed between the bars, but its body, being larger, could not get through, so there it was held fast. The soldier drew an arrow, and, fitting it into the string, shot the snake in the head. Its head being fatally injured, the creature died. The archer then drew it out, pounded it into a pulp, and left it.

A little time later the man's wife conceived and bore a son. From the first the child was afraid of its father, and when it saw him it used to cry and seem greatly frightened. As it grew it hated the sight of its father more and more. The man became suspicious of this, and so, instead of loving his son, he grew to dislike him.

On a certain day, when there were just the two of them in the room, the officer lay down to have a midday siesta, covering his face with his sleeve, but all the while keeping his eye on the boy to see what he would do. The child glared at his father, and thinking him asleep, got a knife and made a thrust at him. The man jumped, grabbed the knife, and then with a club gave the boy a blow that left him dead on the spot. He pounded him into a pulp, left him and went away. The mother, however, in tears, covered the little form with a quilt and prepared for its burial. In a little the quilt began to move, and she in alarm raised it to see what had happened, when lo! beneath it the child was gone and there lay coiled a huge snake instead. The mother jumped back in fear, left the room and did not again enter.

When evening came the husband returned and heard the dreadful story from his wife. He went in and looked, and now all had metamorphosed into a huge snake. On the head of it was the scar mark of the arrow that he had shot. He said to the snake, "You and I were originally not enemies, I therefore did wrong in shooting you as I did; but your intention to take revenge through becoming my son was a horrible deed. Such a thing as this is proof that my suspicions of you were right and just. You became my son in order to kill me, your father; why, therefore, should I not in my turn kill you? If you attempt it again, it will certainly end in my taking your life. You have already had your revenge, and have once more transmigrated into your original shape, let us drop the past and be friends from now on. What do you say?"

He repeated this over and urged his proposals, while the snake with bowed head seemed to listen intently. He then opened the door and said, "Now you may go as you please." The snake then departed, making straight for the Water Gate, and passed out between the bars. It did not again appear.

Note.- Man is a spiritual being, and different from all other created things, and though a snake has power of venom, it is still an insignificant thing compared with a man. The snake died, and by means of the transmigration of its soul took its revenge. Man dies, but I have never heard that he can transmigrate as the snake did. Why is it that though a spiritual being he is unable to do what beasts do? I have seen many innocent men killed, but not one of them has ever returned to take his revenge on the lawless one who did it, and so I wonder more than ever over these stories of the snake. The Superior Man's knowing nothing of the law that governs these things is a regret to me.

THE BRAVE MAGISTRATE

In olden times in one of the counties of North Ham-kyong Province, there was an evil-smelling goblin that caused great destruction to life. Successive magistrates appeared, but in ten days or so after arrival, in each case they died in great agony, so that no man wished to have the billet or anything to do with the place. A hundred or more were asked to take the post, but they all refused. At last one brave soldier, who was without any influence socially or politically, accepted. He was a courageous man, strong and fearless. He thought, "Even though there is a devil there, all men will not die, surely. I shall make a trial of him." So he said his farewell, and entered on his office. He found himself alone in the yamen, as all others had taken flight. He constantly carried a long knife at his belt, and went thus armed, for he noticed from the first day a fishy, stinking odor, that grew gradually more and more marked.

After five or six days he took note, too, that what looked like a mist would frequently make its entry by the outer gate, and from this mist came this stinking smell. Daily it grew more and more annoying, so that he could not stand it longer. In ten days or so, when the time arrived for him to die, the yamen-runners and servants, who had returned, again ran away. The magistrate kept a jar of whisky by his side, from which he drank frequently to fortify his soul. On this day he grew very drunk, and thus waited. At last he saw something coming through the main gateway that seemed wrapped in fog, three or four embraces in waist size, and fifteen feet or so high. There was no head to it, nor were body or arms visible. Only on the top were two dreadful eyes rolling wildly. The magistrate jumped up at once, rushed toward it, gave a great shout and struck it with his sword. When he gave it the blow there was the sound of thunder, and the whole thing dissipated. Also the foul smell that accompanied it disappeared at once.

The magistrate then, in a fit of intoxication, fell prone. The retainers, all thinking him dead, gathered in the courtyard to prepare for his burial. They saw him fallen to the earth, but they remarked that the bodies of others who had died from this evil had all been left on the verandah, but his was in the lower court. They raised him up in order to repare him for burial, when suddenly he came to life, looked at them in anger, and asked what they meant. Fear and amazement possessed them. From that time on there was no more smell.

THE TEMPLE TO THE GOD OF WAR

Yi Hang-bok.- When he was a child a blind fortune-teller came and cast his future, saying, "This boy will be very great indeed."

At seven years of age his father gave him for subject to write a verse on "The Harp and the Sword," and he wrote-

"The Sword pertains to the Hand of the Warrior

And the Harp to the Music of the Ancients."

At eight he took the subject of the "Willow before the Door," and wrote-

"The east wind brushes the brow of the cliff

And the willow on the edge nods fresh and green."

On seeing a picture of a great banquet among the fierce Turks of Central Asia, he wrote thus-

"The hunt is off in the wild dark hills,

And the moon is cold and gray,

While the tramping feet of a thousand horse

Ring on the frosty way.

In the tents of the Turk the music thrills

And the wine-cups chink for joy,

158

'Mid the noise of the dancer's savage tread
And the lilt of the wild hautboy."

At twelve years of age he was proud, we are told, and haughty. He dressed well, and was envied by the poorer lads of the place, and once he took off his coat and gave it to a boy who looked with envy on him. He gave his shoes as well, and came back barefoot. His mother, wishing to know his mind in the matter, pretended to reprimand him, but he replied, saying, "Mother, when others wanted it so, how could I refuse giving?" His mother pondered these things in her heart.

When he was fifteen he was strong and well-built, and liked vigorous exercise, so that he was a noted wrestler and skilful at shuttlecock. His mother, however, frowned upon these things, saying that they were not dignified, so that he gave them up and confined his attention to literary studies, graduating at twenty-five years of age.

In 1592, during the Japanese War, when the King escaped to Eui-ju, Yi Hang-bok went with him in his flight, and there he met the Chinese (Ming) representative, who said in surprise to his Majesty, "Do you mean to tell me that you have men in Cho-sen like Yi Hang-bok?" Yang Ho, the general of the rescuing forces, also continually referred to him for advice and counsel. He lived to see the troubles in the reign of the wicked Kwang-hai, and at last went into exile to Puk-chong. When he crossed the Iron Pass near Wonsan, he wrote-

"From the giddy height of the Iron Peak,
I call on the passing cloud,
To take up a lonely exile's tears
In the folds of its feathery shroud,
And drop them as rain on the Palace Gates,
On the King, and his shameless crowd."

The Story

During the Japanese War in the reign of Son-jo, the Mings sent a great army that came east, drove out the enemy and restored peace. At that time the general of the Mings informed his Korean Majesty that the victory was due to the help of Kwan, the God of War. "This being the case," said he, "you ought not to continue without temples in which to express your gratitude to him." So they built him houses of worship and offered him sacrifice. The Temples built were one to the south and one to the east of the city. In examining sites for these they could not agree on the one to the south. Some wanted it nearer the wall and some farther away. At that time an official, called Yi Hang-bok, was in charge of the conference. On a certain day when Yi was at home a military officer called and wished to see him. Ordering him in he found him a great strapping fellow, splendidly built. His request was that Yi should send out all his retainers till he talked to him privately. They were sent out, and then the stranger gave his message. After he had finished, he said good-bye and left.

Yi had at that time an old friend stopping with him. The friend went out with the servants when they were asked to leave, and now he came back again. When he came in he noticed that the face of the master had a very peculiar expression, and he asked him the reason of it. Yi made no reply at first, but later told his friend that a very extraordinary thing had happened. The military man who had come and called was none other than a messenger of the God of War. His coming, too, was on account of their not yet having decided in regard to the site for the Temple. "He came," said Yi, "to show me where it ought to be. He urged that it was not a matter for time only, but for the eternities to come. If we do not get it right the God of War will find no peace. I told him in reply that I would do my best. Was this not strange?"

The friend who heard this was greatly exercised, but Yi warned him not to repeat it to anyone. Yi used all his efforts, and at last the building was placed on the approved site, where it now stands.

A VISIT FROM THE SHADES

Choi Yu-won.- (The story of meeting his mother's ghost is reported to be of this man.)

Choi Yu-won matriculated in 1579 and graduated in 1602, becoming Chief Justice and having conferred on him the rank of prince. When he was a boy his great-aunt once gave him cloth for a suit of clothes, but he refused to accept of it, and from this his aunt prophesied that he would yet become a famous man. He studied in the home of the great teacher Yul-gok, and Yul-gok also foretold that the day would come when he would be an honor to Korea.

Yu-won once met Chang Han-kang and inquired of him concerning Pyon-wha Keui-jil (a law by which the weak became strong, the wicked good, and the stupid wise). He also asked that if one be truly transformed will the soul change as well as the body, or the body only? Chang replied, "Both are changed, for how could the body change without the soul?" Yu-won asked Yul-gok concerning this also, and Yul-gok replied that Chang's words were true.

In 1607 Choi Yu-won memorialized the King, calling attention to a letter received from Japan in answer to a communication sent by his Majesty, which had on its address the name of the Prime Minister, written a space lower than good form required. The Korean envoy had not protested, as duty would require of him, and yet the King had advanced him in rank. The various officials commended him for his courage.

In 1612, while he was Chief Justice, King Kwang-hai tried to degrade the Queen Dowager, who was not his own mother, he being born of a concubine, but Yu-won besought him with tears not to do so illegal and unnatural a thing. Still the King overrode all opposition, and did according to his unfilial will. In it all Choi Yu-won was proven a good man and a just. He used to say to his companions, even as a youth, "Death is dreadful, but still, better death for righteousness' sake and honor than life in disgrace." Another saying of his runs, "All one's study is for the development of character; if it ends not in that it is in vain."

Korea's ancient belief was that the blood of a faithful son served as an elixir of life to the dying, so that when his mother was at the point of death Yu-won with a knife cut flesh from his thigh till the blood flowed, and with this he prepared his magic dose.

The Story

There was a minister in olden days who once, when he was Palace Secretary, was getting ready for office in the morning. He had on his ceremonial dress. It was rather early, and as he leaned on his arm-rest for a moment, sleep overcame him. He dreamt, and in the dream he thought he was mounted and on his journey. He was crossing the bridge at the entrance to East Palace Street, when suddenly he saw his mother coming towards him on foot. He at once dismounted, bowed, and said, "Why do you come thus, mother, not in a chair, but on foot?"

She replied, "I have already left the world, and things are not where I am as they are where you are, and so I walk."

The secretary asked, "Where are you going, please?"

She replied, "We have a servant living at Yong-san, and they are having a witches' prayer service there just now, so I am going to partake of the sacrifice."

"But," said the secretary, "we have sacrificial days, many of them, at our own home, those of the four seasons, also on the first and fifteenth of each month. Why do you go to a servant's house and not to mine?"

The mother replied, "Your sacrifices are of no interest to me, I like the prayers of the witches. If there is no medium we spirits find no satisfaction. I am in a hurry," said she, "and cannot wait longer," so she spoke her farewell and was gone.

The secretary awoke with a start, but felt that he had actually seen what had come to pass.

He then called a servant and told him to go at once to So-and-So's house in Yong-san, and tell a certain servant to come that night without fail. "Go quickly," said the secretary, "so that you can be back before I enter the Palace." Then he sat down to meditate over it.

In a little the servant had gone and come again. It was not yet broad daylight, and because it was cold the servant did not enter straight, but went first into the kitchen to warm his hands before the fire. There was a fellow-servant there who asked him, "Have you had something to drink?"

He replied, "They are having a big witch business on at Yong-san, and while the mutang (witch) was performing, she said that the spirit that possessed her was the mother of the master here. On my appearance she called out my name and said, 'This is a servant from our house.' Then she called me and gave me a big glass of spirit. She added further, 'On my way here I met my son going into the Palace.'"

The secretary, overhearing this talk from the room where he was waiting, broke down and began to cry. He called in the servant and made fuller inquiry, and more than ever he felt assured that his mother's spirit had really gone that morning to share in the koot (witches' sacrificial ceremony).

He then called the mutang, and in behalf of the spirit of his mother made her a great offering. Ever afterwards he sacrificed to her four times a year at each returning season.

THE FEARLESS CAPTAIN

There was formerly a soldier, Yee Man-ji of Yong-nam, a strong and muscular fellow, and brave as a lion. He had green eyes and a terrible countenance. Frequently he said, "Fear! What is fear?" On a certain day when he was in his house a sudden storm of rain came on, when there were flashes of lightning and heavy claps of thunder. At one of them a great ball of fire came tumbling into his home and went rolling over the verandah, through the rooms, into the kitchen and out into the yard, and again into the servants' quarters. Several times it went and came bouncing about. Its blazing light and the accompanying noise made it a thing of terror.

Yee sat in the outer verandah, wholly undisturbed. He thought to himself, "I have done no wrong, therefore why need I fear the lightning?" A moment later a flash struck the large elm tree in front of the house and smashed it to pieces. The rain then ceased and the thunder likewise.

Yee turned to see how it fared with his family, and found them all fallen senseless. With the greatest of difficulty he had them restored to life. During that year they all fell ill and died, and Yee came to Seoul and became a Captain of the Right Guard. Shortly after he went to North Ham-kyong Province. There he took a second wife and settled down. All his predecessors had died of goblin influences, and the fact that calamity had overtaken them while in the official quarters had caused them to use one of the village houses instead.

Yee, however, determined to live down all fear and go back to the old quarters, which he extensively repaired.

One night his wife was in the inner room while he was alone in the public office with a light burning before him. In the second watch or thereabout, a strange-looking object came out of the inner quarters. It looked like the stump of a tree wrapped in black sackcloth. There was no outline or definite shape to it, and it came jumping along and sat itself immediately before Yee Man-ji. Also two other objects came following in its wake, shaped just like the first one. The three then sat in a row before Yee, coming little by little closer and closer to him. Yee moved away till he had backed up against the wall and could go no farther. Then he said, "Who are you, anyhow; what kind of devil, pray, that you dare to push towards me so in my office? If you have any complaint or matter to set right, say so, and I'll see to it."

The middle devil said in reply, "I'm hungry, I'm hungry, I'm hungry."

Yee answered, "Hungry, are you? Very well, now just move back and I'll have food prepared for you in abundance." He then repeated a magic formula that he had learned, and snapped his fingers. The three devils seemed to be afraid of this. Then Man-ji suddenly closed his fist and struck a blow at the first devil. It dodged, however, most deftly and he missed, but hit the floor a sounding blow that cut his hand.

Then they all shouted, "We'll go, we'll go, since you treat guests thus." At once they bundled out of the room and disappeared.

On the following day he had oxen killed and a sacrifice offered to these devils, and they returned no more.

Note.- Men have been killed by goblins. This is not so much due to the fact that goblins are wicked as to the fact that men are afraid of them. Many died in North Ham-kyong, but those again who were brave, and clove them with a knife, or struck them down, lived. If they had been afraid, they too would have died.

THE KING OF YOM-NA (HELL)

Pak Chom was one of the Royal Censors, and died in the Japanese War of 1592.

The Story

In Yon-nan County, Whang-hai Province, there was a certain literary graduate whose name I have forgotten. He fell ill one day and remained in his room, leaning helplessly against his arm-rest. Suddenly several spirit soldiers appeared to him, saying, "The Governor of the lower hell has ordered your arrest," so they bound him with a chain about his neck, and led him away. They journeyed for many hundreds of miles, and at last reached a place that had a very high wall. The spirits then took him within the walls and went on for a long distance.

There was within this enclosure a great structure whose height reached to heaven. They arrived at the gate, and the spirits who had him in hand led him in, and when they entered the inner courtyard they laid him down on his face.

Glancing up he saw what looked like a king seated on a throne; grouped about him on each side were attendant officers. There were also scores of secretaries and soldiers going and coming on pressing errands. The King's appearance was most terrible, and his commands such as to fill one with awe. The graduate felt the perspiration break out on his back, and he dared not look up. In a little a secretary came forward, stood in front of the raised dais to transmit commands, and the King asked, "Where do you come from? What is your name? How old are you? What do you do for a living? Tell me the truth now, and no dissembling."

The scholar, frightened to death, replied, "My clan name is So-and-so, and my given name is So-and-so. I am so old, and I have lived for several generations at Yon-nan, Whang-hai Province. I am stupid and ill-equipped by nature, so have not done anything special. I have heard all my life that if you say your beads with love and pity in your heart you will escape hell, and so have given my time to calling on the Buddha, and dispensing alms."

The secretary, hearing this, went at once and reported it to the King. After some time he came back with a message, saying, "Come up closer to the steps, for you are not the person intended. It happens that you bear the same name and you have thus been wrongly arrested. You may go now."

The scholar joined his hands and made a deep bow. Again the secretary transmitted a message from the King, saying, "My house, when on earth, was in such a place in such and such a ward of Seoul. When you go back I want to send a message by you. My coming here is long, and the outer coat I wear is worn to shreds. Ask my people to send me a new outer coat. If you do so I shall be greatly obliged, so see that you do not forget."

The scholar said, "Your Majesty's message given me thus direct I shall pass on without fail, but the ways of the two worlds, the dark world and the light, are so different that when I give the message the hearers will say I am talking nonsense. True, I'll give it just as you have commanded, but what about it if they refuse to listen? I ought to have some evidence as proof to help me out."

The King made answer, "Your words are true, very true. This will help you: When I was on earth," said he, "one of my head buttons1 that I wore had a broken edge, and I hid it in the third volume of the Book of History. I alone know of it, no one else in the world. If you give this as a proof they will listen."

173

The scholar replied, "That will be satisfactory, but again, how shall I do in case they make the new coat?"

The reply was, "Prepare a sacrifice, offer the coat by fire, and it will reach me."

He then bade good-bye, and the King sent with him two soldier guards. He asked the soldiers, as they came out, who the one seated on the throne was. "He is the King of Hades," said they; "his surname is Pak and his given name is Oo."

They arrived at the bank of a river, and the two soldiers pushed him into the water. He awoke with a start, and found that he had been dead for three days.

When he recovered from his sickness he came up to Seoul, searched out the house indicated, and made careful inquiry as to the name, finding that it was no other than Pak Oo. Pak Oo had two sons, who at that time had graduated and were holding office. The graduate wanted to see the sons of this King of Hades, but the gatekeeper would not let him in. Therefore he stood before the red gate waiting helplessly till the sun went down. Then came out from the inner quarters of the house an old servant, to whom he earnestly made petition that he might see the master. On being thus requested, the servant returned and reported it to the master, who, a little later, ordered him in. On entering, he saw two gentlemen who seemed to be chiefs. They had him sit down, and then questioned him as to who he was and what he had to say

He replied, "I am a student living in Yonnan County, Whang-hai Province. On such and such a day I died and went into the other world, where your honorable father gave me such and such a commission."

The two listened for a little and then, without waiting to hear all that he had to say, grew very angry and began to scold him, saying, "How dare such a scarecrow as you come into our house and say such things as these? This is stuff and nonsense that you talk. Pitch him out," they shouted to the servants.

He, however, called back saying, "I have a proof; listen. If it fails, why then, pitch me out."

One of the two said, "What possible proof can you have?" Then the scholar told with great exactness and care the story of the head button.

The two, in astonishment over this, had the book taken down and examined, and sure enough in Vol. III of the Book of History was the button referred to. Not a single particular had failed. It proved to be a button that they had missed after the death of their father, and that they had searched for in vain.

Accepting the message now as true, they all entered upon a period of mourning.

The women of the family also called in the scholar and asked him specially of what he had seen. So they made the outer coat, chose a day, and offered it by fire before the ancestral altar. Three days after the sacrifice the scholar dreamed, and the family of Pak dreamed too, that the King of Hades had come and given to each one of them his thanks for the coat. They long kept the scholar at their home, treating him with great respect, and became his firm friends for ever after.

Pak Oo was a great-grandson of Minister Pak Chom. While he held office he was honest and just and was highly honored by the people. When he was Mayor of Hai-ju there arose a dispute between him and the Governor, which proved also that Pak was the honest man.

When I was at Hai-ju, Choi Yu-chom, a graduate, told me this story.

The head button is the insignia of rank, and is consequently a valuable heirloom in a Korean home.- J. S. G.

HONG'S EXPERIENCES IN HADES

Hong Nai-pom was a military graduate who was born in the year A.D. 1561, and lived in the city of Pyeng-yang. He passed his examination in the year 1603, and in the year 1637 attained to the Third Degree. He was 82 in the year 1643, and his son Sonn memorialized the King asking that his father be given rank appropriate to his age. At that time a certain Han Hong-kil was chief of the Royal Secretaries, and he refused to pass on the request to his Majesty; but in the year 1644, when the Crown Prince was returning from his exile in China, he came by way of Pyeng-yang. Sonn took advantage of this to present the same request to the Crown Prince. His Highness received it, and had it brought to the notice of the King. In consequence, Hong received the rank of Second Degree.

On receiving it he said, "This year I shall die," and a little later he died.

In the year 1594, Hong fell ill of typhus fever, and after ten days of suffering, died. They prepared his body for burial, and placed it in a coffin. Then the friends and relatives left, and his wife remained alone in charge. Of a sudden the body turned itself and fell with a thud to the ground. The woman, frightened, fainted away, and the other members of the family came rushing to her help. From this time on the body resumed its functions, and Hong lived.

Said he, "In my dream I went to a certain region, a place of great fear where many persons were standing around, and awful ogres, some of them wearing bulls' heads, and some with faces of wild beasts. They crowded about and jumped and pounced toward me in all directions. A scribe robed in black sat on a platform and addressed me, saying, 'There are three religions on earth, Confucianism, Buddhism and Taoism. According to Buddhism, you know that heaven and hell are places that decide between man's good and evil deeds. You have ever been a blasphemer of the Buddha, and a denier of a future life, acting always as though you knew everything, blustering and storming. You are now to be sent to hell, and ten thousand kalpas1 will not see you out of it.'

"Then two or three constables carrying spears came and took me off. I screamed, 'You are wrong, I am innocently condemned.' Just at that moment a certain Buddha, with a face of shining gold, came smiling toward me, and said, 'There is truly a mistake somewhere; this man must attain to the age of eighty-three and become an officer of the Second Degree ere he dies.' Then addressing me he asked, 'How is it that you have come here? The order was that a certain Hong of Chon-ju be arrested and brought, not you; but now that you have come, look about the place before you go, and tell the world afterwards of what you have seen.'

"The guards, on hearing this, took me in hand and brought me first to a prison-house, where a sign was posted up, marked, 'Stirrers up of Strife.' I saw in this prison a great brazier-shaped pit, built of stones and filled with fire. Flames arose and forked tongues. The stirrers up of strife were taken and made to sit close before it. I then saw one infernal guard take a long rod of iron, heat it red-hot, and put out the eyes of the guilty ones. I saw also that the offenders were hung up like dried fish. The guides who accompanied me, said, 'While these were on earth they did not love their brethren, but looked at others as enemies. They scoffed at the laws of God and sought only selfish gain, so they are punished.'

"The next hell was marked, 'Liars.' In that hell I saw an iron pillar of several yards in height, and great stones placed before it. The offenders were called up, and made to kneel before the pillar. Then I saw an executioner take a knife and drive a hole through the tongues of the offenders, pass an iron chain through each, and hang them to the pillar so that they dangled by their tongues several feet from the ground. A stone was then taken and tied to each culprit's feet. The stones thus bearing down, and the chains being fast to the pillar, their tongues were pulled out a foot or more, and their eyes rolled in their sockets. Their agonies were appalling. The guides again said, 'These offenders when on earth used their tongues skillfully to tell lies and to separate friend from friend, and so they are punished.'

"The next hell had inscribed on it, 'Deceivers.' I saw in it many scores of people. There were ogres that cut the flesh from their bodies, and fed it to starving demons. These ate and ate, and the flesh was cut and cut till only the bones remained. When the winds of hell blew, flesh returned to them; then metal snakes and copper dogs crowded in to bite them and suck their blood. Their screams of pain made the earth to tremble. The guides said to me, 'When these offenders were on earth they held high office, and while they pretended to be true and good they received bribes in secret and were doers of all evil. As Ministers of State they ate the fat of the land

and sucked the blood of the people, and yet advertised themselves as benefactors and were highly applauded. While in reality they lived as thieves, they pretended to be holy, as Confucius and Mencius are holy. They were deceivers of the world, and robbers, and so are punished thus.'

"The guides then said, 'It is not necessary that you see all the hells.' They said to one another, 'Let's take him yonder and show him;' so they went some distance to the south-east. There was a great house with a sign painted thus, 'The Home of the Blessed.'

As I looked, there were beautiful haloes encircling it, and clouds of glory. There were hundreds of priests in cassock and surplice. Some carried fresh-blown lotus flowers; some were seated like the Buddha; some were reading prayers.

"The guides said, 'These when on earth kept the faith, and with undivided hearts served the Buddha, and so have escaped the Eight Sorrows and the Ten Punishments, and are now in the home of the happy, which is called heaven.' When we had seen all these things we returned.

"The golden-faced Buddha said to me, 'Not many on earth believe in the Buddha, and few know of heaven and hell. What do you think of it?'

"I bowed low and thanked him.

"Then the black-coated scribe said, 'I am sending this man away; see him safely off.' The spirit soldiers took me with them, and while on the way I awakened with a start, and found that I had been dead for four days."

Hong's mind was filled with pride on this account, and he frequently boasted of it. His age and Second Degree of rank came about just as the Buddha had predicted.

His experience, alas! was used as a means to deceive people, for the Superior Man does not talk of these strange and wonderful things.

Yi Tan, a Chinaman of the Song Kingdom, used to say, "If there is no heaven, there is no heaven, but if there is one, the Superior Man alone can attain to it. If there is no hell, there is no hell, but if there is one the bad man must inherit it."

If we examine Hong's story, while it looks like a yarn to deceive the world, it really is a story to arouse one to right action. I, , have recorded it like Toi-chi, saying, "Don't find fault with the story, but learn its lesson."

Kalpa means a Buddhist age.

HAUNTED HOUSES

There once lived a man in Seoul called Yi Chang, who frequently told as an experience of his own the following story: He was poor and had no home of his own, so he lived much in quarters loaned him by others. When hard pressed he even went into haunted houses and lived there. Once, after failing to find a place, he heard of one such house in Ink Town (one of the wards of Seoul), at the foot of South Mountain, which had been haunted for generations and was now left vacant. Chang investigated the matter, and finally decided to take possession.

First, to find whether it was really haunted or not, he called his elder brothers, Hugh and Haw, and five or six of his relatives, and had them help clean it out and sleep there. The house had one upper room that was fast locked. Looking through a chink, there was seen to be in the room a tablet chair and a stand for it; also there was an old harp without any strings, a pair of worn shoes, and some sticks and bits of wood. Nothing else was in the room. Dust lay thick, as though it had gathered through long years of time.

The company, after drinking wine, sat round the table and played at games, watching the night through. When it was late, towards midnight, they suddenly heard the sound of harps and a great multitude of voices, though the words were mixed and unintelligible. It was as though many people were gathered and carousing at a feast. The company then consulted as to what they should do. One drew a sword and struck a hole through the partition that looked into the tower. Instantly there appeared from the other side a sharp blade thrust out towards them. It was blue in color. In fear and consternation they desisted from further interference with the place. But the sound of the harp and the revelry kept up till the morning. The company broke up at daylight, withdrew from the place, and never again dared to enter.

In the South Ward there was another haunted house, of which Chang desired possession, so he called his friends and brothers once more to make the experiment and see whether it was really haunted or not. On entering, they found two dogs within the enclosure, one black and one tan, lying upon the open verandah, one at each end. Their eyes were fiery red, and though the company shouted at them they did not move. They neither barked nor bit. But when midnight came these two animals got up and went down into the court, and began baying at the inky sky in a way most ominous. They went jumping back and forth. At that time, too, there came some one round the corner of the house dressed in ceremonial robes. The two dogs met him with great delight, jumping up before and behind in their joy at his coming. He ascended to the verandah, and sat down. Immediately five or six multi-colored demons appeared and bowed before him, in front of the open space. The man then led the demons and the dogs two or three times round the house. They rushed up into the verandah and jumped down again into the court; backwards and forwards they came and went, till at last all of them mysteriously disappeared. The devils went into a hole underneath the floor, while the dogs went up to their quarters and lay down.

The company from the inner room had seen this. When daylight came they examined the place, looked through the chinks of the floor, but saw only an old, worn-out sieve and a few discarded brooms. They went behind the house and found another old broom poked into the chimney. They ordered a servant to gather them up and have them burned. The dogs lay as they were all day long, and neither ate nor moved. Some of the party wished to kill the brutes, but were afraid, so fearsome was their appearance.

This night again they remained, desiring to see if the same phenomena would appear. Again at midnight the two dogs got down into the court and began barking up at the sky. The man in ceremonial robes again came, and the devils, just as the day before.

The company, in fear and disgust, left the following morning, and did not try it again.

A friend, hearing this of Chang, went and asked about it from Hugh and Haw, and they confirmed the story.

There is still another tale of a graduate who was out of house and home and went into a haunted dwelling in Ink Town, which was said to have had the tower where the mysterious sounds were heard. They opened the door, broke out the window, took out the old harp, the spirit chair, the shoes and sticks, and had them burned. Before the fire had finished its work, one of the servants fell down and died. The graduate, seeing this, in fear and dismay put out the fire, restored the things and left the house.

Again there was another homeless man who tried it. In the night a woman in a blue skirt came down from the loft, and acted in a peculiar and uncanny way. The man, seeing this, picked up his belongings and left.

Again, in South Kettle Town, there were a number of woodmen who in the early morning were passing behind the haunted house, when they found an old woman sitting weeping under a tree. They thinking her an evil bogey, one man came up behind and gave her a thrust with his sickle. The witch rushed off into the house, her height appearing to be only about one cubit and a span.

IM, THE HUNTER

I'm Kyong-up.- One of Korea's most famous generals, who fought in behalf of China in 1628 against the Manchus. He is worshipped to-day in many parts of Korea.

The Story

When General I'm Kyong-up was young he lived in the town of Tallai. In those days he loved the chase, and constantly practised riding and hunting. Once he went off on an excursion to track the deer in Wol-lak Mountains. He carried only a sword, and made the chase on foot. In his pursuit of the animal he went as far as Tai-paik Mountain. There night overtook him, and the way was hidden in the darkness. There were yawning chasms and great horns and cliffs on all sides. While he was in a state of perplexity he met a woodman, and asked him where the road was and how he ought to go. The woodman directed him to a cliff opposite, "where," said he, "there is a house." I'm heard this and crossed over to the farther ridge. On approaching more nearly he found a great tiled mansion standing alone without a single house about it. He went in by the main gateway, but found all quiet and dark and no one in sight. It was a vacant house, evidently deserted. After travelling all day in the hills I'm was full of fears and creepy feelings. So he viewed the place with mistrust, fearing that there might be hill goblins in it or tree devils, but a moment later someone opened the room door and shouted out, "Do you sleep here? Have you had something to eat?"

I'm looked and discovered that it was the same person that had directed him on his way. He said in reply, "I have not eaten anything and am hungry." So the man opened the wall box and brought him out wine and meat. He, being exceedingly hungry, ate all. Then they sat down to talk together, and after a little the woodman got up, opened the box once more, and took from it a great sword. I'm asked, "What is this you have; do you intend to kill me?"

The woodman laughed and said, "No, no, but to-night there is something on hand worth the seeing. Will you come with me and not be afraid?"

I'm said, "Of course I am not afraid; I want to see."

It was then about midnight, and the woodman, with the sword in his hand, took I'm and went to one side through a succession of gates that seemed never ending. At last they came to a place where lights were reflected on a pond of water. There was a high pavilion apparently in the middle of the lake, and from the inside of it came the lights. There were sounds, too, of laughter and talking that came from the upper storey. Through the sliding doors he could distinguish two people seated together. There was another pavilion to the right of the lake and a large tree near it, up which the woodman told I'm to climb.

"When you get well up," said he, "take your belt, tie yourself fast to the trunk and keep perfectly still."

I'm climbed the tree as directed, and made himself secure. From this point of vantage he looked intently, and the first thing he saw was the woodman give a leap that cleared the lake and landed him in the pavilion. At once he ascended to the upper storey, and now I'm could distinguish three persons sitting talking and laughing. He heard the woodman, after drinking, say to his neighbor, "We have made our wager, now let's see it out." The man replied, "Let's do so." Then both arose, came down to the entrance, and vaulted off into mid-air, where they disappeared from sight. Nothing could be distinguished now but the clashing of steel and flashes of fire, which kept up for a long time.

In beholding this from the tree top, where he was stationed, his bones grew cold and his hair stood stiff on end. He knew not what to do. Then a moment later he heard something fall to the ground with a great thud. A cry of victory arose too, and he recognized that it was the woodman's voice. Chills ran all over him, and goose-flesh covered his skin; only after a long time could he gain control of himself. He came down from the tree and the woodman met him, took him suddenly under his arm, and vaulted over into the pavilion. Here he met a beautiful woman with hair like fleecy clouds. Before the fight the woman's voice was evidently full of hilarity, but now she was overcome with grief and tears.

The woodman spoke roughly to her, saying, "Do you not know that you, a wicked woman, have caused the death of a great man?" The woodman said also to I'm, "You have courage and valour in your way, but it is not sufficient to meet a world like this. I will now give you this woman, and this house, so you can bid farewell to the dusty world and live here in peace and quiet for the rest of your days."

I'm replied, "What I have seen to-night I am at a loss to understand. I'd like to know the meaning of it first; please tell me. After hearing that I'll do what you ask."

The woodman said, "I am not an ordinary mortal of the world, but am an outlaw of the hills and woods. I am a robber, really, and by robbing have many such a house as this. Not only here but in all the provinces I have homes abundant, a beautiful woman in each, and rich and dainty fare. All unexpectedly this woman has neglected me for another man, and he and she have several times tried to kill me. There being no help for it, I had to kill him. I have killed the man, but I ought truly to have killed the woman. Take this place, then, off my hands, will you, and the woman too?"

But I'm asked, "Who was the man, and where did he live?"

"There were," said the woodman, "mighty possibilities in him, though he lived humbly inside the South Gate of Seoul and sold cut tobacco. He came here frequently, and I knew it, though I winked at it all until they attempted to kill me, and that brought matters to a head. It was not my wish to kill him," and here the woodman broke down and cried. "Alas, alas!" said he, "I have killed a great and

193

gifted man. Think it over," said he; "you have courage, but not enough to make any mark in the world. You will fail half-way, the Fates have so decided. Cease from any vain ambitions, for there is no way by which your name can ever become famous. Do what I say, then, and take over this woman and this home."

I'm, however, shook his head and said, "I can't do it."

The woodman asked, "Why can you not? If you do not, there is nothing for this woman but death, so here I'll have done with it," and he struck her with his sword and cut off her head.

The day following he said to I'm, "Since you are determined to go forth and do valiantly, I cannot stop you, but if a man goes forth thus and does not know the use of the sword he is helpless, and at the mercy of the foe. Stay with me a little and learn. I'll teach you."

I'm stayed for six days and learned the use of the sword.

THE MAGIC INVASION OF SEOUL

A gentleman of Seoul was one day crossing the Han River in a boat. In the crossing, he nodded for a moment, fell asleep and dreamed a dream. In his dream he met a man who had Gothic eyebrows and almond eyes, whose face was red as ripened dates, and whose height was eight cubits and a span. He was dressed in green and had a long beard that came down to his belt-string. A man of majestic appearance he was, with a great sword at his side and he rode on a red horse.

He asked the gentleman to open his hand, which he did, and then the august stranger dashed a pen-mark on it as the sign of the God of War. Said he, "When you cross the river, do not go direct to Seoul, but wait at the landing. Seven horses will shortly appear, loaded with network hampers, all proceeding on their journey to the capital. You are to call the horsemen, open your hand, and show them the sign. When they see it they will all commit suicide in your very presence. After that, you are to take the loads and pile them up, but don't look into them. Then you are to go at once and report the matter to the Palace and have them all burned. The matter is of immense importance, so do not fail in the slightest particular."

The gentleman gave a great start of terror and awoke. He looked at his hand and there, indeed, was the strange mark. Not only so, but the ink had not yet dried upon it. He was astonished beyond measure, but did as the dream had indicated, and waited on the river's bank. In a little there came, as he was advised, the seven loads on seven horses, coming from the far-distant South. There were attendants in charge, and one man wearing an official coat came along behind. When they had crossed the river the gentleman called them to him and said, "I have something to say to you; come close to me." These men, unsuspecting, though with somewhat of a frightened look, closed up. He then showed them his hand with the mark, and asked them if they knew what it was. When they saw it, first of all, the man in the official coat turned and with one bound jumped over the cliff into the river. The eight or nine who accompanied the loads likewise all rushed after him and dashed into the water.

The scholar then called the boatmen, and explained to them that the things in the hampers were dangerous, that he would have to make it known to the Palace, and that in the meantime they were to keep close guard, but that they were not to touch them or look at them.

He hurried as fast as possible, and reported the matter to the Board of War. The Board sent an official, and had the loads brought into Seoul, and then, as had been directed, they were piled high with wood and set on fire. When the fire developed, the baskets broke open, and little figures of men and horses, each an inch or so long, in countless numbers, came tumbling out.

When the officials saw this they were frozen with fear; their hearts ceased beating and their tongues lolled out. In a little, however, the hampers were all burned up.

These were the creation of a magician, and were intended for a monster invasion of Seoul, until warned by Kwan.

From that time on the people of Seoul began faithful offerings to the God of War, for had he not saved the city?

THE AWFUL LITTLE GOBLIN

There was an occasion for a celebration in the home of a nobleman of Seoul, whereupon a feast, to which were invited all the family friends, was prepared. There was a great crowd of men and women. In front of the women's quarters there suddenly appeared an uncombed, ugly-looking boy about fifteen years of age. The host and guests, thinking him a coolie who had come in the train of some visitor, did not ask specially concerning him, but one of the women guests, seeing him in the inner quarters, sent a servant to reprimand him and put him out. The boy, however, did not move, so the servant said to him, "Who are you, anyway, and with whom did you come, that you enter the women's quarters, and even when told to go out do not go?"

The boy, however, stood stock-still, just as he had been, with no word of reply.

The company looked at him in doubt, and began to ask one another whose he was and with whom he had come. Again they had the servant make inquiry, but still there was no reply. The women then grew very angry, and ordered him to be put out. Several took hold of him and tried to pull him, but he was like a fixed rock, fast in the earth, absolutely immovable. In helpless rage they informed the men.

The men, hearing this, sent several strong servants, who took hold all at once, but he did not budge a hair. They asked, "Who are you, anyway?" but he gave no reply. The crowd, then enraged, sent ten strong men with ropes to bind him, but like a giant mountain he remained fast, so that they recognized that he could not be moved by man's power.

One guest remarked, "But he, too, is human; why cannot he be moved?" They then sent five or six giant fellows with clubs to smash him to pieces, and they laid on with all their might. It looked as though he would be crushed like an egg-shell, while the sound of their pounding was like reverberating thunder. But just as before, not a hair did he turn, not a wink did he give.

Then the crowd began to fear, saying, "This is not a man, but a god," so they entered the courtyard, one and all, and began to bow before him, joining their hands and supplicating earnestly. They kept this up for a long time.

At last the boy gave a sarcastic smile, turned round, went out of the gate and disappeared.

The company, frightened out of their wits, called off the feast. From that day on, the people of that house were taken ill, including host and guests. Those who scolded him, those who tied him with ropes, those who pounded him, all died in a few days. Other members of the company, too, contracted typhus and the like, and died also.

It was commonly held that the boy was the Too-uk Spirit, but we cannot definitely say. Strange, indeed!

Note.- When the time comes for a clan to disappear from the earth, calamity befalls it. Even though a great spirit should come in at the door at such a feast time, if the guests had done as Confucius suggests, "Be reverent and distant," instead of insulting him and making him more malignant than ever, they would have escaped. Still, devils and men were never intended to dwell together.

GOD'S WAY

In a certain town there lived a man of fierce and ungovernable disposition, who in moments of anger used to beat his mother. One day this parent, thus beaten, screamed out, "Oh, God, why do you not strike dead this wicked man who beats his mother?"

The beating over, the son thrust his sickle through his belt and went slowly off to the fields where he was engaged by a neighbor in reaping buckwheat. The day was fine, and the sky beautifully clear. Suddenly a dark fleck of cloud appeared in mid-heaven, and a little later all the sky became black. Furious thunder followed, and rain came on. The village people looked out toward the field, where the flashes of lightning were especially noticeable. They seemed to see there a man with lifted sickle trying to ward them off. When the storm had cleared away, they went to see, and lo, they found the man who had beaten his mother struck dead and riven to pieces.

God takes note of evil doers on this earth, and deals with them as they deserve. How greatly should we fear!

THE OLD MAN IN THE DREAM

Kwon Jai was a man high in rank and well advanced in years. He was, however, much given to sport and various kinds of pleasure. One night he had a dream, when an old man came to him, who bowed low, and in tears said, "Sir, Minister Hong wishes to kill off me and all my posterity. Please save me, won't you?"

Kwon asked, "How can I save you?" The old man replied, "Hong will assuredly ask Your Excellency to help him. Desist from it, please, for if you do, Hong will give it up and I shall live and all mine."

A little later there came a rap at the door, when Kwon awakened and asked, "Who is there?" It was Hong, who that day had planned an excursion to Lotus Lake to fish for turtles, and now had come specially to invite Kwon to go with him.

Then Kwon knew that the turtle had appeared to him in a dream in the form of an old man, so he declined, saying he was ill. I learned later that Hong also did not go.

THE PERFECT PRIEST

There was once a priest called Namnu who had perfected his ways in the Buddhist doctrine. Whenever he had clothing of his own he would willingly undress and give it to those who were cold. His spirit was gentle with no creases or corners in it. Everybody, high and low, rich and poor, called him by the nickname of Softy. Whenever he saw any one sentenced to a flogging in the temple or official yamen, Namnu invariably begged that he might take the culprit's place. Once, when there was a great function in progress at Pagoda Temple and many high officials were assembled, Softy, too, was seen kneeling at the side and taking part. He suddenly remarked to Prince Hong of Yon-san, "You are indeed a very great man."

Hong replied, "What do you mean by 'great man,' you impudent brat? Take that," and he gave him a box with his fist on the ear. Softy laughed, and said, "Please, Hong, don't do that, it hurts! it hurts!"

Later I was in the train of Prince Yi of Yun-song, and other high officials were present, when we stopped for a little before the Temple. Softy was there, and he looked at Yi and said, "I know your face, but I have forgotten your name." Afterwards he said, "Oh, I remember now, you are Yi Sok-hyong." The priests of the monastery who heard this familiarity were scandalized, and hurried to make no end of apology to the Prince, saying, "Softy was born so, God made him so. Please, Your Excellency, forgive him." The Prince forgave him and so he was not disturbed.

THE PROPITIOUS MAGPIE

People say that when the magpie builds its nest directly south of a home that the master of the house will be promoted in office. King T'ai-jong had a friend once who was very poor and had failed in all his projects. After various fruitless attempts he decided to wait till the King went out on procession and then to send a servant to build an imitation magpie's nest in some propitious place before him. The King saw it and asked the man what he was doing. He said in reply that when a magpie builds its nest straight south of a home the master of the house instantly gets promotion. His master, he said, had waited so long and nothing had come, that he was building an imitation nest to bring it about. The King took pity on him and ordered his appointment at once.

When I was young myself a magpie built its nest before our home, but I, along with other boys, cut off the branch so that the whole nest fell to the ground, and there were the young with their pitiful yellow mouths. I felt sorry and afraid that they would die, so on a propitious site to the south I had the nest hung up on a neutie tree, where the young all lived and flourished and flew away. In that very winter my father was promoted three degrees in rank and was attached to the office of the Prime Minister.

Afterwards I built a summer-house at Chong-pa, and before the house, directly facing south, magpies built a nest in a date tree. I had a woman slave, and she pulled it down and used the nest for fuel, but they came again the next year and built once more. The year following was 1469 when Ye-jong came to the throne. That year again I was promoted. In the spring of 1471 magpies came and built their nest in a tree just south of my office. I laughed and said, "There is a spiritual power in the magpie surely, as men have said from olden times and as I myself have proven."

THE "OLD BUDDHA"

Prime Minister Choi Yun-tok was in mourning once for his mother. With a single horse and one servant he made a journey to the south where the road led through the county of Kai-ryong. At that very time two or three of the district magistrates had pitched a tent on the bank of the river and were having refreshments. They said to one another, "Who is that mourner that goes riding by without dismounting? It must be some country farmer who has never learned proper manners. We shall certainly have to teach him a lesson."

They sent an attendant to arrest and bring his servant, whom they asked, "Who is your master?"

He replied, "Choi, the Old Buddha."

"But what's his real name?" they demanded.

"The old Buddha," was the reply.

Then they grew very angry at this, and said, "Your master has offended in not dismounting, and you offend in concealing his name. Both slave and master are equally ill-mannered." And so they beat him over the head.

Then the servant said slowly, "He is called Choi the Buddha, but his real name is Yun-tok, and he is now on his way to his country home in Chang-won." At once they recognized that it was no other than the Prime Minister, and great fear overcame them. They struck their tent, cleared away the eatables, and ran to make their deepest salaam and to ask pardon for their sin.

The old Buddha was a special name by which this famous minister was known.

A WONDERFUL MEDICINE

Prince Cheung had been First Minister of the land for thirty years. He was a man just and upright, now nearly ninety years of age. His son was called Whal, and was second in influence only to his father. Both were greatly renowned in the age in which they lived, and His Majesty treated them with special regard. Prince Cheung's home was suddenly attacked by goblins and devils, and when a young official came to call on him, these mysterious beings in broad daylight snatched the hat from his head and crumpled it up. They threw stones, too, and kept on throwing them so that all the court was reduced to confusion. Prince Cheung made his escape and went to live in another house, where he prepared a special medicine called sal-kwi-whan (kill-devil-pills), which he offered in prayer. From that time the goblins departed, and now after five or six years no sign of them has reappeared. Prince Cheung, too, is well and strong and free from sickness.

FAITHFUL MO

Prince Ha had a slave who was a landed proprietor and lived in Yang-ju county. He had a daughter, fairest of the fair, whom he called Mo(Nobody), beautiful beyond expression. An Yun was a noted scholar, a man of distinction in letters. He saw Mo, fell in love with her and took her for his wife. Prince Ha heard of this and was furiously angry. Said he, "How is it that you, a slave, dare to marry with a man of the aristocracy?" He had her arrested and brought home, intending to marry her to one of his bondsmen. Mo learned of this with tears and sorrow, but knew not what to do. At last she made her escape over the wall and went back to An. An was delighted beyond expression to see her; but, in view of the old prince, he knew not what to do. Together they took an oath to die rather than to be parted.

Later Prince Ha, on learning of this, sent his underlings to arrest her again and carry her off. After this all trace of her was lost till Mo was discovered one day in a room hanging by the neck dead.

Months of sorrow passed over An till once, under cover of the night, he was returning from the Confucian Temple to his house over the ridge of Camel Mountain. It was early autumn and the wooded tops were shimmering in the moonlight. All the world had sunk softly to rest and no passers were on the way. An was just then musing longingly of Mo, and in heartbroken accents repeating love verses to her memory, when suddenly a soft footfall was heard as though coming from among the pines. He took careful notice and there was Mo. An knew that she was long dead, and so must have known that it was her spirit, but because he was so buried in thought of her, doubting nothing, he ran to her and caught her by the hand, saying, "How did you come here?" but she disappeared. An gave a great cry and broke into tears. On account of this he fell ill. He ate, but his grief was so great he could not swallow, and a little later he died of a broken heart.

Kim Champan, who was of the same age as I, and my special friend, was also a cousin of An, and he frequently spoke of this. Yu Hyo-jang, also, An's nephew by marriage, told the story many times. Said he, "Faithful unto death was she. For even a woman of the literati, who has been born and brought up at the gates of ceremonial form, it is a difficult matter enough to die, but for a slave, the lowest of the low, who knew not the first thing of Ceremony, Righteousness, Truth or Devotion, what about her? To the end, out of love for her husband, she held fast to her purity and yielded up her life without a blemish. Even of the faithful among the ancients was there ever a better than Mo?"

THE RENOWNED MAING

Minister of State Maing Sa-song once upon a time, dressed in plain clothes, started south on a long journey. On the way he was overtaken by rain, and turned into a side pavilion for rest and shelter. There was a young scholar already in the pavilion by the name of Whang Eui-hon, who with his two hands behind his back was reading the pavilion inscription board, on which verses were written. Long he read and long he looked about as though no one else were there. At last he turned to the old man, and said, "Well, grand-dad, do you know the flavor of verses like these?" The famous Minister, pretending ignorance, arose and said, "An old countryman like myself, could you expect him to know? Please tell me the meaning."

Whang said, "These verses were written by the great men of the past. What they saw and experienced they wrote down to inspire the souls of those who were to come after them. They are like pictures of sea and land, for there are living pictures in poetry, you know."

The Minister said, "Indeed, that's wonderful; but if it were not for men like yourself how should I ever come to know these things?"

A little later came pack-horses loaded with all sorts of things; servants and retainers, too, a great company of them, tent poles, canvas packs and other equipment, a long procession.

Whang, surprised by this, made inquiry, when, to his amazement, he learned that the old man was none other than Maing Sa-song. Unconsciously he dropped on to his knees in a deep and long obeisance. The Minister laughed and said, "That will do; there is no difference in the value of mere men, they are high or low according to the thoughts that prompt them, but unfortunately all are born with a proud heart. You are not a common scholar, why, therefore, should you be so proud to begin with and so humble now?" The Minister took him by the hand, led him to his mat, made him sit down, comforted him and sent him away.

THE SENSES

The eyes are round like gems, so that they can roll about and see things; the ears have holes in them so that they can hear; the nose has openings by which it can perceive smell; and the mouth is horizontal and slit so that it can inhale and exhale the breath; the tongue is like an organ reed so that it can make sounds and talk. Three of the four have each their particular office to fulfill, while the mouth has two offices. But the member that distinguishes the good from the bad is the heart, so that without the heart, even though you have eyes you cannot see, though you have ears you cannot hear, though you have a nose you cannot smell, and though you have a mouth you cannot breathe, so they say that without the heart "seeing you cannot see, and hearing you cannot hear."

WHO DECIDES, GOD OR THE KING?

King Tai-jong was having a rest in Heung-yang Palace, while outside two eunuchs were talking together over the law that governs the affairs of men, as to whether it is man or God. A said, "Riches and honor are all in the king's hand." B said, "Nothing of the kind; every atom of wealth and every degree of promotion are all ordered of God. Even the king himself has no part in it and no power."

So they argued, each that he was right, without ever coming to an agreement.

The King, overhearing what was said, wrote a secret dispatch, saying, "Raise the Bearer of this letter one degree in rank." He sealed it and commanded A to take it to Se-jong, who was then in charge of this office. A made his bow and departed, but just when he was about to leave the palace enclosure a furious pain took him in the stomach, so that he begged B to take his place and go into the city.

The next day, when the record of promotions was placed before the King, he read how B had been advanced, but not one word was there about A.

King Tai-jong made inquiry, and when he knew the circumstances he gave a sudden start of wonder and remained long in deep thought.

THREE THINGS MASTERED

There was a relative of the king, named I'm Sung-jong, who was a gifted man in thought and purpose. He was the first performer of his time on the harp. King Se-jong said of him, "Im's harp knows but one master, and follows no other man."

His home was outside the South Gate, and every morning he was seen kneeling on the sill of his front door beating his hands upwards and downwards on his knees, and this practice he carried on for three years. People could not imagine what he meant by it, but thought him mad. Thus he learned the motions required for the harp.

Also he blew with his mouth and practised with his fingers day and night without stopping, so that when people called on him he would see them but would not perceive them. He kept this up for three years and so learned the motions for the flute.

He was a lightly built man in body, and poor at riding and at archery. He often sighed over this defect, and said, "Though I am weak and stupid and not able to shoot a long distance, I shall yet know how to hit the target and make the bull's-eye. This also must be acquired by practice." So every morning he took his bow and arrows and went off into the hills. There he shot all day long, keeping it up for three years, till he became a renowned archer. Thus you may perceive the kind of man he was.

STRANGELY STRICKEN DEAD

There was once a man called Kim Tok-saing, a soldier of fortune, who had been specially honored at the Court of Tai-jong. He had several times been generalissimo of the army, and on his various campaigns had had an intimate friend accompany him, a friend whom he greatly loved. But Kim had been dead now for some ten years and more, when one night this friend of his was awakened with a start and gave a great outcry. He slept again, but a little later was disturbed once more by a fright, at which he called out. His wife, not liking this, inquired as to what he meant. The friend said, "I have just seen General Kim riding on a white horse, with bow and arrows at his belt. He called to me and said, 'A thief has just entered my home, and I have come to shoot him dead.' He went and again returned, and as he drew an arrow from his quiver, I saw that there were blood marks on it. He said, 'I have just shot him, he is dead.'" The husband and wife in fear and wonder talked over it together.

When morning came the friend went to General Kim's former home to make inquiry. He learned that that very night Kim's young widow had decided to remarry, but as soon as the chosen fiancé had entered her home, a terrible pain shot him through, and before morning came he died in great agony.

THE MYSTERIOUS HOI TREE

Prince Pa-song's house was situated just inside of the great East Gate, and before it was a large Hoi tree. On a certain night the Prince's son-in-law was passing by the roadway that led in front of the archers' pavilion. There he saw a great company of bowmen, more than he could number, all shooting together at the target. A moment later he saw them practicing riding, some throwing spears, some hurling bowls, some shooting from horseback, so that the road in front of the pavilion was blocked against all comers. Some shouted as he came by, "Look at that impudent rascal! He attempts to ride by without dismounting." They caught him and beat him, paying no attention to his cries for mercy, and having no pity for the pain he suffered, till one tall fellow came out of their serried ranks and said in an angry voice to the crowd, "He is my master; why do you treat him so?" He undid his bonds, took him by the arm and led him home. When the son-in-law reached the gate he looked back and saw the man walk under the Hoi tree and disappear. He then learned, too, that all the crowd of archers were spirits and not men, and that the tall one who had befriended him was a spirit too, and that he had come forth from their particular Hoi tree.

TA-HONG

Sim Heui-su studied as a young man at the feet of No Su-sin, who was sent as an exile to a distant island in the sea. Thither he followed his master and worked at the Sacred Books. He matriculated in 1570 and graduated in 1572. In 1589 he remonstrated with King Son-jo over the disorders of his reign, and was the means of quelling a great national disturbance; but he made a faux pas one day when he said laughingly to a friend-

"These sea-gull waves ride so high,
Who can take them?"

Those who heard caught at this, and it became a source of unpopularity, as it indicated an unfavorable opinion of the Court.

In 1592, when the King made his escape to Eui-ju, before the invading Japanese army, he was the State's Chief Secretary, and after the return of the King he became Chief Justice. He resigned office, but the King refused to accept his resignation, saying, "I cannot do without you." He became chief of the literati and Special Adviser. Afterwards he became Minister of the Right, then of the Left, at which time he wrote out ten suggestions for His Majesty to follow. He saw the wrongs done around the King, and resigned office again and again, but was constantly recalled.

In 1608 I'm Suk-yong, a young candidate writing for his matriculation, wrote an essay exposing the wrongs of the Court. Sim heard of this, and took the young man under his protection. The King, reading the essay, was furiously angry, and ordered the degradation of I'm, but Sim said, "He is with me; I am behind what he wrote and approve; degrade me and not him," and so the King withdrew his displeasure. He was faithful of the faithful.

When he was old he went and lived in Tun-san in a little tumble-down hut, like the poorest of the literati. He called himself "Water-thunder Muddy-man," a name derived from the Book of Changes.

He died in 1622 at the age of seventy-four, and is recorded as one of Korea's great patriots.

The Story

Minister Sim Heui-su was, when young, handsome as polished marble, and white as the snow, rarely and beautifully formed. When eight years of age he was already an adept at the character, and a wonder in the eyes of his people. The boy's nickname was Soondong (the godlike one). From the passing of his first examination, step by step he advanced, till at last he became First Minister of the land. When old he was honored as the most renowned of all ministers. At seventy he still held office, and one day, when occupied with the affairs of State, he suddenly said to those about him, "To-day is my last on earth, and my farewell wishes to you all are that you may prosper and do bravely and well."

His associates replied in wonder, "Your Excellency is still strong and hearty, and able for many years of work; why do you speak so?"

Sim laughingly made answer, "Our span of life is fixed. Why should I not know? We cannot pass the predestined limit. Please feel no regret. Use all your efforts to serve His Majesty the King, and make grateful acknowledgment of his many favors."

Thus he exhorted them, and took his departure. Every one wondered over this strange announcement. From that day on he returned no more, it being said that he was ailing.

There was at that time attached to the War Office a young secretary directly under Sim. Hearing that his master was ill, the young man went to pay his respects and to make inquiry. Sim called him into his private room, where all was quiet. Said he, "I am about to die, and this is a long farewell, so take good care of yourself, and do your part honorably."

The young man looked, and in Sim's eyes were tears. He said, "Your Excellency is still vigorous, and even though you are slightly ailing, there is surely no cause for anxiety. I am at a loss to understand your tears, and what you mean by saying that you are about to die. I would like to ask the reason."

Sim smiled and said, "I have never told any person, but since you ask and there is no longer cause for concealment, I shall tell you the whole story. When I was young certain things happened in my life that may make you smile.

"At about sixteen years of age I was said to be a handsome boy and fair to see. Once in Seoul, when a banquet was in progress and many dancing-girls and other representatives of good cheer were called, I went too, with a half-dozen comrades, to see. There was among the dancing-girls a young woman whose face was very beautiful. She was not like an earthly person, but like some angelic being. Inquiring as to her name, some of

227

those seated near said it was Ta-hong (Flower-bud).

"When all was over and the guests had separated, I went home, but I thought of Ta-hong's pretty face, and recalled her repeatedly, over and over; seemingly I could not forget her. Ten days or so later I was returning from my teacher's house along the main street, carrying my books under my arm, when I suddenly met a pretty girl, who was beautifully dressed and riding a handsome horse. She alighted just in front of me, and to my surprise, taking my hand, said, 'Are you not Sim Heui-su?'

"In my astonishment I looked at her and saw that it was Ta-hong. I said, 'Yes, but how do you know me?' I was not married then, nor had I my hair done up, and as there were many people in the street looking on I was very much ashamed. Flower-bud, with a look of gladness in her face, said to her pony-boy, 'I have something to see to just now; you return and say to the master that I shall be present at the banquet to-morrow.' Then we went aside into a neighboring house and sat down. She said, 'Did you not on such and such a day go to such and such a Minister's house and look on at the gathering?' I answered, 'Yes, I did.' 'I saw you,' said she, 'and to me your face was like a god's. I asked those present who you were, and they said your family name was Sim and your given-name Heui-su, and that your character and gifts were very superior. From that day on I longed to meet you, but as there was no possibility of this I could only think of you. Our meeting thus is surely of God's appointment.'

"I replied laughingly, 'I, too, felt just the same towards you.'

"Then Ta-hong said, 'We cannot meet here; let's go to my aunt's home in the next ward, where it's quiet, and talk there.' We went to the aunt's home. It was neat and clean and somewhat isolated, and apparently the aunt loved Flower-bud with all the devotion of a mother. From that day forth we plighted our troth together. Flower-bud had never had a lover; I was her first and only choice. She said, however, 'This plan of ours cannot be consummated to-day; let us separate for the present and make plans for our union in the future.' I asked her how we could do so, and she replied, 'I have sworn my soul to you, and it is decided forever, but you have your parents to think of, and you have not yet had a wife chosen, so there will be no chance of their advising you to have a second wife as my social standing would require for me. As I reflect upon your ability and chances for promotion, I see you already a Minister of State. Let us separate just now, and I'll keep myself for you till the time when you win the first place at the Examination and have your three days of public rejoicing. Then we'll meet once more. Let us make a compact never to be broken. So then, until you have won your honors, do not think of me, please. Do not be anxious, either, lest I should be taken from you, for I have a plan by which to hide myself away in safety. Know that on the day when you win your honors we shall meet again.'

"On this we clasped hands and spoke our farewells as though we parted easily. Where she was going I did not ask, but simply came home with a distressed and burdened heart, feeling that I had lost everything. On my return I found that my parents, who had missed me, were in a terrible state of consternation, but so delighted were they at my safe return that they scarcely asked where I had been. I did not tell them either, but gave another excuse.

"At first I could not desist from thoughts of Ta-hong. After a long time only was I able to regain my composure. From that time forth with all my might I went at my lessons. Day and night I pegged away, not for the sake of the Examination, but for the sake of once more meeting her.

"In two years or so my parents appointed my marriage. I did not dare to refuse, had to accept, but had no heart in it, and no joy in their choice.

"My gift for study was very marked, and by diligence I grew to be superior to all my competitors. It was five years after my farewell to Ta-hong that I won my honors. I was still but a youngster, and all the world rejoiced in my success. But my joy was in the secret understanding that the time had come for me to meet Ta-hong. On the first day of my graduation honors I expected to meet her, but did not. The second day passed, but I saw nothing of her, and the third day was passing and no word had reached me. My heart was so disturbed that I found not the slightest joy in the honors of the occasion. Evening was falling, when my father said to me, 'I have a friend of my younger days, who now lives in Chang-eui ward, and you must go and call on him this evening before the three days are over,' and so, there being no help for it, I went to pay my call. As I was returning the sun had gone down and it was dark, and just as I was passing a high gateway, I heard the Sillai call.1 It was the home of an old Minister, a man whom I did not know, but he being a high noble there was nothing for me to do but to dismount and enter. Here I found the master himself, an old gentleman, who put me through my humble exercises, and then ordered me gently to come up and sit beside him. He talked to me very kindly, and entertained me with all sorts of refreshments. Then he lifted his glass and inquired, 'Would you like to meet a very beautiful person?' I did not know what he meant, and so asked, 'What beautiful person?' The old man said, 'The most beautiful in the world to you. She has long been a member of my household.' Then he ordered a servant to call her. When she came it was my lost Ta-hong. I was startled, delighted, surprised, and speechless almost. 'How do you come here?' I gasped.

"She laughed and said, 'Is this not within the three days of your public celebration, and according to the agreement by which we parted?'

"The old man said, 'She is a wonderful woman. Her thoughts are high and noble, and her history is quite unique. I will tell it to you. I am an old man of eighty, and my wife and I have had no children, but on a certain day this young girl came to us saying, "May I have the place of slave with you, to wait on you and do your bidding?"

"'In surprise I asked the reason for this strange request, and she said, "I am not running away from any master, so do not mistrust me."

"'Still, I did not wish to take her in, and told her so, but she begged so persuasively that I yielded and let her stay, appointed her work to do, and watched her behavior. She became a slave of her own accord, and simply lived to please us, preparing our meals during the day, and caring for our rooms for the night; responding to calls; ever ready to do our bidding; faithful beyond compare. We feeble old folks, often ill, found her a source of comfort and cheer unheard of, making life perfect peace and joy. Her needle, too, was exceedingly skilful, and according to the seasons she prepared all that we needed. Naturally we loved and pitied her more than I can say. My wife thought more of her than ever mother did of a daughter. During the day she was always at hand, and at night she slept by her side. At one time I asked her quietly concerning her past history. She said she was originally the child of a free-man, but that her parents had died when she was very young, and, having no place to go to, an old woman of the village had taken her in and brought her up. "Being so young," said she, "I was safe from harm. At last I met a young master with whom I plighted a hundred years of troth, a beautiful boy, none was ever like him. I determined to meet him again, but only after he had won his honors in the arena. If I had remained at the home of the old mother I could not have kept myself safe, and preserved my honor; I would have been helpless; so I came here for safety and to serve you. It is a plan by which to hide myself for a year or so, and then when he wins I shall ask your leave to go."

"'I then asked who the person was with whom she had made this contract, and she told me your name. I am so old that I no longer think of taking wives and concubines, but she called herself my concubine so as to be safe, and thus the years have passed. We watched the Examination reports, but till this time your name was absent. Through it all she expressed not a single word of anxiety, but kept up heart saying that before long your name would appear. So confident was she that not a shadow of disappointment was in her face. This time on looking over the list I found your name, and told her. She heard it without any special manifestation of joy, saying she knew it would come. She also said, "When we parted I promised to meet him before the three days of public celebration were over, and now I must make good my promise." So she climbed to the upper pavilion to watch the public way. But this ward being somewhat remote she did not see you going by on the first day, nor on the second. This morning she went again, saying, "He will surely pass to-day"; and so it came about. She said, "He is coming; call him in."

"'I am an old man and have read much history, and have heard of many famous women. There are many examples of devotion that move the heart, but I never saw so faithful a life nor one so devoted to another. God taking note of this has brought all her purposes to pass. And now, not to let this moment of joy go by, you must stay with me to-night.'

"When I met Ta-hong I was most happy, especially as I heard of her years of faithfulness. As to the invitation I declined it, saying I could not think, even though we had so agreed, of taking away one who waited in attendance upon His Excellency. But the old man laughed, saying, 'She is not mine. I simply let her be called my concubine in name lest my nephews or some younger members of the clan should steal her away. She is first of all a faithful woman: I have not known her like before.'

"The old man then had the horse sent back and the servants, also a letter to my parents saying that I would stay the night. He ordered the servants to prepare a room, to put in beautiful screens and embroidered matting, to hang up lights and to decorate as for a bridegroom. Thus he celebrated our meeting.

"Next morning I bade good-bye, and went and told my parents all about my meeting with Ta-hong and what had happened. They gave consent that I should have her, and she was brought and made a member of our family, really my only wife.

"Her life and behavior being beyond that of the ordinary, in serving those above her and in helping those below, she fulfilled all the requirements of the ancient code. Her work, too, was faithfully done, and her gifts in the way of music and chess were most exceptional. I loved her as I never can tell.

"A little later I went as magistrate to Keumsan county in Chulla Province, and Ta-hong went with me. We were there for two years. She declined our too frequent happy times together, saying that it interfered with efficiency and duty. One day, all unexpectedly, she came to me and requested that we should have a little quiet time, with no others present, as she had something special to tell me. I asked her what it was, and she said to me, 'I am going to die, for my span of life is finished; so let us be glad once more and forget all the sorrows of the world.' I wondered when I heard this. I could not think it true, and asked her how she could tell beforehand that she was going to die. She said, 'I know, there is no mistake about it.'

"In four or five days she fell ill, but not seriously, and yet a day or two later she died. She said to me when dying, 'Our life is ordered, God decides it all. While I lived I gave myself to you, and you most kindly responded in return. I have no regrets. As I die I ask only that my body be buried where it may rest by the side of my master when he passes away, so that when we meet in the regions beyond I shall be with you once again.' When she had so said she died.

"Her face was beautiful, not like the face of the dead, but like the face of the living. I was plunged into deepest grief, prepared her body with my own hands for burial. Our custom is that when a second wife dies she is not buried with the family, but I made some excuse and had her interred in our family site in the county of Ko-yang. I did so to carry out her wishes. When I came as far as Keum-chang on my sad journey, I wrote a verse-

'O beautiful Bud, of the beautiful Flower,
We bear thy form on the willow bier;
Whither has gone thy sweet perfumed soul?
The rains fall on us
To tell us of thy tears and of thy faithful way.'

"I wrote this as a love tribute to my faithful Ta-hong. After her death, whenever anything serious was to happen in my home, she always came to tell me beforehand, and never was there a mistake in her announcements. For several years it has continued thus, till a few days ago she appeared in a dream saying, 'Master, the time of your departure has come, and we are to meet again. I am now making ready for your glad reception.'

"For this reason I have bidden all my associates' farewell. Last night she came once more and said to me, 'To-morrow is your day.' We wept together in the dream as we met and talked. In the morning, when I awoke, marks of tears were still upon my cheeks. This is not because I fear to die, but because I have seen my Ta-hong. Now that you have asked me I have told you all. Tell it to no one." So Sim died, as was foretold, on the day following. Strange, indeed!

241

Made in the USA
Monee, IL
09 June 2020

33005233R00138